Peirene

ANDREA LUNDGREN

TRANSLATED FROM THE SWEDISH
BY JOHN LITELL

Nordisk fauna

AUTHOR

Andrea Lundgren was born in 1986 and grew up in Boden, in the far north of Sweden. Her debut novel, *I tunga vintrars mage*, was published in 2010 and was followed in 2014 by *Glupahungern*. *Nordisk Fauna*, her first short-story collection, was published in 2018. It was awarded the 2018 Tidningen Vi's Literature Prize and was nominated for the 2018 Svenska Dagbladet's Literature Award and the 2019 Norrland Literature Prize. This is the first of Lundgren's works to be translated into English.

TRANSLATOR

John Litell is a physician and translator from Swedish to English. He grew up just north of Stockholm and now lives in Minneapolis, USA, where he also serves on the board of trustees of the American Swedish Institute. He is the winner of the 2020 Peirene Stevns Translation Prize. *Nordic Fauna* is his debut literary translation, which he completed while working in intensive care throughout the Covid-19 pandemic.

First published in Great Britain in 2021 by
Peirene Press Ltd
17 Cheverton Road
London N19 3BB
www.peirenepress.com

First published under the original Swedish-language title *Nordisk Fauna* by Natur & Kultur

Published by arrangement with Partners in Stories Stockholm, Sweden

With special thanks to Sarah Death, who offered editorial support and guidance as part of the Peirene Stevns Translation Prize mentorship.

ISBN 978-1-908670-63-2

Designed by Sacha Davison Lunt

Cover illustration: Caroline McArthur

Typeset by Tetragon, London
Printed and bound by T J International, Padstow, Cornwall

The translation of this work was supported by the Peirene Stevns Translation Prize, which was established with the generous support of Martha Stevns in 2018.

Supported using public funding by
**ARTS COUNCIL
ENGLAND**

Peirene

ANDREA LUNDGREN

TRANSLATED FROM THE SWEDISH
BY JOHN LITELL

Nordic Fauna

God is not the limit of man, but the limit of man is divine. In other words, man is divine in the experience of his limits.

GEORGES BATAILLE

... for it is given some to come out of their skins, and for others to dwindle therein ...

DJUNA BARNES,
Ryder

Of course I don't dispute that a chasm separates the soul from the world, but I am convinced that at the very bottom of that chasm sooner or later there is always a glimpse of the possibility that there will arise a new, heretofore unimagined symbiosis between the world and the soul, which will leave neither of them in its previously unaffected state.

LÁSZLÓ F. FÖLDÉNYI,
*The Glance of the
Medusa: The Physiognomy
of Mysticism*

Contents

The Bird That Cries in the Night

When I reach the edge of the slope I see him down on the thin strip of riverbank that forms a boundary against the deepening water. He is wearing his grey-blue windcheater with the turquoise stripe down each side, the one he's had for ages. The sun has reached its highest point in the sky and it casts a dazzling band across the water. Shades of yellow and orange have crept into the maples and Dad stands there, toiling away in the underbrush. It surrounds him almost completely – raspberry thickets, bird cherry shrubs, rowan saplings. The hedge trimmer rests against a splintered stump. He bends down, grasps a fistful of thistles and pulls. A shake to loosen the largest clods of soil and then he tosses the weeds into the wheelbarrow. The water glitters in the sunshine and across Dad's brow. When he notices me standing there above him he straightens his back and wipes the sweat from his face with one of his gardening gloves.

*

'I couldn't sleep last night,' he tells me when we've reached the kitchen.

He makes coffee and I sink onto the bench seat. The upholstery is worn. When I was little I used to lie there on my belly with my homework, idly stroking the floral pattern. It's a little pilled and in some places the foam shows through.

'Why not?'

He takes a seat opposite me. The tabletop around his right hand is stained with water rings.

'Some bird was calling from down by the river. About four in the morning. Loudly.'

'What kind of bird?'

He reaches across the table for the folded newspaper and thumbs through it, although I know he's read it already. He has doodled something in the corner of the crossword page. A silhouette of a bird, like the top of a totem pole. Smiling, I angle my head slightly to get a better view, but he moves on.

'Well, not one I've ever heard before,' he says. 'Two quick calls in a row. *Wiiiiip, wiiiiip*. Over and over like a siren. I just couldn't get back to sleep so I went outside.'

'Did you see it?'

'No. It was probably further down, towards the bridge.'

He gets to his feet and fetches the coffee pot, fills my cup and then his own. I say something about milk and get up to have a look in the fridge. A few strands of hair cling to sticky spots on the glass shelves. But there is food too: a few open tins, an onion, a sausage with some rice porridge. I sit back down. His eyes are pale blue and carry a tired loneliness, like those of an elderly husky. His hand trembles slightly as he lifts the translucent cup to his lips. His mother's china. He only brings it out when I come round. Otherwise he always uses a big mug from his old job. It's two years since he had to quit. He blamed his back, said it was better now but that there wasn't any point in returning. Too much running around, he said. I'm done with all that.

'It must've been a crane,' I offer, letting a half spoonful of sugar slowly tumble into my cup.

I don't know why I do it. I always take my coffee without, always black, at least four cups a day, and I won't take a drop of milk, not since I watched a documentary that showed a calf crying for its mother for days on end. There was no need for it any more, not for me. I stopped immediately. And that was years before I even started drinking coffee, when I was sixteen, in the school cafeteria by one of the big windows. I could sit there all by myself and stare at the dying foliage.

'It wasn't a crane,' he says without looking up from the paper. 'A sea eagle, maybe.'

His finger traces the newspaper columns; one of his cheeks occasionally twitches. He has a bit of stubble, which makes him look old. He used to be so meticulous, early in the morning before work. The shaving foam resembled whipped cream.

He asks me how I'm doing, how it's going at work. I tell him I'm all right, that it's going well. I take occasional swallows of my sweetened coffee and steal glances at him. His face is thinner than mine; I have Mum's high cheekbones, her grey eyes. But my back is his, hunched over indoors but straight and strong when I go out. For a long time I couldn't bring myself to wear button-up shirts because they just reminded me of him. It was as though I was dressed in his skin. Now that's all I wear. At the same time it's strange to come out here, like travelling back in time, every metre of country road rolling back a few weeks of my life, and I grow shorter as I go. And it's so quiet here. Speaking just makes it worse.

'I read that you can get cancer from working nights,' he says. 'It's in the paper.'

I can see the side of the cup through the top few millimetres of coffee but the bottom is thick with grounds. He glances through the radio schedule. He used to listen to *Classical Morning*, getting up before me and Mum. One time I walked in on him in the middle of an aria. I was probably eight years old; it was winter and pitch-black outside. I must've been on my way to the toilet, wearing just my underwear, half asleep, when I saw him in the kitchen, leaning against the counter with his shoulders drawn back like wings. And this heavenly song, and how he just stood there.

He doesn't let me stay long. We finish our coffee and then he wants to head back down and get on with his work.

'You've never cared about that slope before,' I say, standing on the paving stones leading up to the road, rooting around in my jacket pockets for the car keys.

'You can see for yourself how overgrown it's getting,' he says. 'It makes me so restless.'

I feel the cold metal against my fingers and gaze across the property. The lone maple reigns over the far end near the slope down to the river. There isn't a single unkempt blade of grass. A few leaves loosen their grasp and descend through the air to the manicured lawn.

'Just don't overexert yourself,' I say calmly.

But it's as though he is already down there by the half-full wheelbarrow; the round stones on the riverbank, the water lapping against them, can already feel his hands closing around the stalks of the thistles, all the way down, against the earth, where he can get the best grip.

On my way up to the car I turn round once and catch sight of him just as he disappears. He walks briskly, as if he's afraid he'll run out of time.

I climb into the car, a little Mazda with grey upholstery and a broken latch on the glove compartment. I lean back but it doesn't feel right. Only a partial view in the mirror and my feet don't quite reach the pedals. I adjust the seat, straighten the mirrors. The windscreen seems greasy, as though someone has systematically pressed their fingers against it, trying to find their way out.

I drive back to town.

'It's a little late to take cuttings now, I know,' Mum says, as she hastily finishes watering the flowers before coming out into the hall and hugging me, still holding the white watering can.

I leave my shoes on the doormat and hang my coat on the hook next to hers.

'How were things with Aron?' she asks from the kitchen.

I hear the clattering of china.

'No coffee for me,' I say as I enter.

She stops herself and instead takes out two glasses.

'I have a little raspberry juice,' she says. 'How does that sound?'

'Great,' I reply. 'He was in the middle of clearing underbrush down by the river. In a bit of a frenzy.'

She fetches the juice mix and stirs it into a jug of water. She has dyed her hair red again; it looks nice with her white cardigan. Her feet move back and forth over the rug on the kitchen floor.

'Do they still make rag rugs,' I ask, 'or are these from Grandma?'

'Of course they still make them.' She takes a container out of the fridge. 'As long as there are rags there will be rag rugs. There will always be things that get old and can be cut up into rags. This one is from my mother. Do you recognize it?'

It is moss green, pale yellow and dark blue. The fringes are braided.

'I don't think so,' I reply.

'Let's go and sit in the living room.'

I follow her through the rounded doorway. The windows are crowded with potted plants, hanging pots and curtains. A few shelves of books that I don't believe she's read but have simply followed her here, because you've got to have bookshelves, no matter what. A little television. A display cabinet and a beautiful old writing desk. Just beside one of the windows is a table covered with cuttings in glasses of water. The living-room table between the sofas is made of medium-brown wood framing a sheet of glass in the centre. There are two matching chairs, but you're not allowed to sit on them because they are likely to break. So they are in storage. She can't get rid of them of course, because they belong with the table.

'Apparently he's been bothered by some bird,' I say as I take a seat on the sofa and pour us each a glass of juice. The colour is wonderful, ruby red.

'Here you go,' Mum says, holding out the plastic tub of biscuits. 'They'll be thawed in a minute.'

I take one and put it on the table. The juice is just the right strength, despite the fact that she prefers to dilute it more. She takes a bite of biscuit and gathers the crumbs with her hand.

'A bird, you say?'

'A sea eagle, he thinks.'

'Ha! More likely a crane. By the way, I read that night shifts can cause cancer.'

I say nothing, running my index finger along the knuckles of the other hand. They are dry, like sandpaper.

'You know, sometimes when I can't sleep I think of how you sit there in that fluorescent light all by yourself.'

'I didn't know you had trouble sleeping,' I say.

'Oh, just every once in a while,' she says. 'Getting old makes you lie there and ruminate.'

The biscuits taste exactly like they did when I was young. They were Dad's favourite; Mum preferred something more substantial, pastries ideally. But we never had those at home. Most often little biscuits with jam. Always those rustic almond biscuits, left over because no one liked them. Every time we had company all the biscuits came out. I loved arranging them on the three-tiered biscuit stand, just like in the bakery. It was mainly Mum's two sisters who came round; Melker hardly ever did, because of his falling-out with Dad a few years earlier. Dad never drank juice, just coffee. One time he found an old cigarette in a cabinet and promptly lit it, just like that. As if he were suddenly somebody else. I didn't even know that Dad had smoked before. Then Mum said, 'God, it smells like smoke in here!' and his expression didn't change in the slightest. I whispered in her ear that it was Dad who had smoked and thought she'd be furious, but he roared with laughter and she laughed too, a new, big laugh, and then she took a seat and they both just sat there and laughed. That was the only time I'd seen Dad smoke.

'How did you and Dad meet?' I ask.

'Oh, you know that story,' she says. 'It was at a party at the hotel and I asked him to dance because my girlfriends had all bet that I wouldn't dare to.'

'And you chose him because he seemed so out of place?'

'Exactly.'

She pours me more juice.

'I definitely can't see Dad at a dance,' I say, and I notice I have a coffee stain on my trousers, shaped like the head of a little bear.

'Everyone danced in those days.'

'Yeah, but still.'

She stands up and walks to the kitchen with her glass. I hear her turn on the tap.

'What's Roger up to today?' I ask once she is back in her armchair.

'We aren't seeing each other any more,' she replies.

'How come?'

'It just ran its course. He didn't like doing things. And you know how I am. Did you know I've started dance lessons?'

'What?'

'Tango. Argentinian, although most of them want to dance Finnish.'

'I didn't even realize there were two kinds.'

'Apparently so. There aren't many men in the group, but I *have* danced with your old school counsellor. Do you remember him? Bengt-Erik?'

'Where do you get the courage?'

She laughs. 'Surely there isn't anything wrong with him?'

'No, no, I just mean, where do you find the courage to take a class like that? Aren't you afraid you'll…'

'Afraid I'll what?'

'I dunno.'

'There's no point in being afraid of things like that. Too much else out there to get worked up about if you really need to – pensions, racists in parliament… You've inherited that shyness from your father.'

I smile crookedly.

'I guess so.'

She quietly watches me as I tie my laces. I stand and pick up the bag of frozen apple sauce she's given me. 'Have it on your porridge,' she said, as though I were the kind of person who made porridge for breakfast, or in fact ate breakfast at all. We hug and I turn to leave.

'Had he tidied up at home?' she asks, and I hesitate. 'Did he seem to be feeling OK?'

I nod.

'And everything's all right with you? Truly?'

There is something wary about her.

'Yes,' I say, waiting for her to continue, but she just nods and we part.

That night I dream about Dad. We are in the shed, branches whip against the windowpanes, there's a storm out on the point, it's night. He is half turned away from me, an orange glow radiates from a lantern on the wall in front of him. The noise outside is deafening. 'Can you hear it beating?' he says, his voice hollow and distant.

I try to look at him but his features are indistinct. It's as if he constantly turns away from me, right at the moment that I almost catch a glimpse of his face. I try to speak but the wind is howling so loudly that I can't hear my own voice.

'What's beating?' I scream. 'What is it that's beating, Dad?'

My legs move heavily towards him but I don't get any closer. Then I see that he's holding something between his cupped hands, something golden. He hunches over it. The light flickers. He presses the secret to his chest and runs headlong out into the storm.

There are safe fathers, I think to myself as I slam the car door in the car park outside work. Fathers who sit in the Sunday morning light and read the newspaper and hum to themselves and then goof around with their kids who sigh and groan, 'Oh, Dad, you just don't get it!' Fathers you can always count on, who tuck you in at night. Then there are the mean ones, who neither have the time nor think you're worthy of it. The ones who try to make a fool of you in front of others, who get drunk and angry and say, 'You're just like your mother.' And then there are fathers like mine. The ones you thought could never handle being on their own. Fathers who mostly sit, and when they're not sitting they're working on something, anything, to keep from suffocating. Then they sit again. The ones who watch television at night even though there's nothing to watch, who go to bed early even though they can't sleep. The ones who never socialize, who don't have friends, maybe just some shamefaced kid who visits far too rarely and doesn't want to anyway because it's so uncomfortable being the only person for someone who doesn't seem to have anything else. The kind of father who is disproportionately glad to see you despite never really having learned how to express his feelings, yet still becomes happy enough for it to be noticeable. What do you do with a father like that? With a mean one you can always try to escape. But you can never quite care enough about a lonely one. Regardless of your efforts, it just feels like all you ever do is leave him.

The pale-yellow light in the hallway makes everything look watered down. Molly sits in the shared changing room, a half-healed cut on her lip, staring into the middle distance, frozen part way through an attempt at buttoning her shirt. As I walk past her she snaps back to life.

'Yo, man,' she says, gathering her hair into a ponytail.

'Yo. That looks lovely.'

She closes her locker and I sit on the bench across from her and start changing.

'I'm just so bloody tired of it,' she says. 'It was Klas, of course. What an arsehole.'

'Mm,' I reply.

He does seem like an arsehole, but that's not something you just say.

'How about you? How are things?'

She stops in the doorway on her way up. Her hair looks like strands of yarn. Last week she told me she had lost 'like, half of it' since she started working here. Twenty-two years old. She must have low stress tolerance.

'One day at a time.'

She nods, presses her lips together slightly, gestures towards the lift and leaves.

Still sitting on the bench, I try flexing one of my sagging biceps but give up almost immediately. My body suddenly feels so heavy. I'm reminded of all the other times I have sat here, every earlier version of this body that has sighed, stood up, closed the locker door and hesitated there briefly, just for a moment, closed its eyes and perhaps glimpsed another life. Just a tiny moment. Never too long – that's dangerous. Becoming one of those people who get stuck gazing into the void is dangerous, because eventually you'll fall apart from being constantly pulled back again. Your arms and legs give way, and then you're lying face down with your nose against the concrete floor, too weak to get up.

I stand up a bit too quickly. When my vision refocuses I'm already halfway to the lift. I don't need eyes to find my way around here.

'Who was that?' Molly asks when I return to the room and pocket my phone.

The old woman between us is so small that she occasionally gets lost among the sheets as we remake her bed. Her name is Agnes and before her health worsened she could joke with the best of them.

'My mother,' I reply, 'calling to remind me that it's my birthday tomorrow.'

'Da-a-amn,' says Molly. 'What are you doing to celebrate?'

'Not sure.' I tuck Agnes in. 'Any suggestions?'

We walk to the next room. Molly first. I follow diagonally behind her, studying the birthmark she has on her neck.

'Do something cool. Skydiving. Everyone I know who's done it says it's, like, the coolest thing they've ever done. Except I guess it can hurt like hell in your ears. From the pressure.'

I grimace.

'Crash into the ground at several hundred kilometres per hour? I'll pass.'

'Suit yourself.'

Molly shrugs.

'I don't get why they can't just buy a little radio for everyone here,' she continues. 'It can't be that expensive. This silence is enough to drive a person crazy.'

'Privatized healthcare,' I reply. 'Hi, Ulrik. How are you feeling today?'

He is seated on his bed, his feet dangling a few centimetres above the floor. Sometimes he turns violent for no clear reason, hurts himself and has to go to A&E. Most of the time he just sits.

'Do you need to use the toilet?'

Molly sits next to him. I turn to the window and pull open the curtains. It has almost no effect. The same pale light. Twilight.

Sometimes I have the urge to just bomb the whole damned place. Level the whole department to the ground. Or just quit and start running in one direction or another until it's easier to breathe. To one of the poles, where the air is clearer than spring water and ice crystals have transformed the world into a glittering expanse that forces you to squint in order to avoid fainting from all the beauty. Where the polar ice cap is several kilometres thick and the snow creaks like an attic door when you walk on it, awkwardly, like a bear cub. And the water, perfectly clean and dark and foreign, can contain just about anything. And you can stand there on the edge of it, lean over and imagine that down there the whales are angels, swimming past window after window for all eternity. Through arch after arch. High up near the surface you can just barely taste a trace of the deep, something unfamiliar in your mouth, a flavour that makes you thirsty. And then you drink. Drink and drink until it sloshes in your stomach and you have a little of that unknown within you. At least then you can be certain that there's more out there than what's visible.

That would be enough.

At lunch I tell Molly that I'm planning to celebrate with a boat ride. It just came to me.

'Where?' she asks, between bites.

'Doesn't really matter. I'm just going out somewhere with a boat.'

'It's *on* a boat.'

'OK, "*on* a boat",' I repeat.

'So you're saying you like boats?'

'I don't think so.' I put down my cutlery and remember something. 'But we had a boat when I was a kid,' I say, trying to grasp the flicker of a memory. 'A little rowing boat.'

'Ah,' says Molly as she starts paging through a magazine.

*

As with any time I try to remember something, it's like glancing over my shoulder and being suddenly blinded by the sun. You can't see a thing, so you turn back with nothing but jagged black spots dancing in your eyes. If I didn't already know that dementia wasn't like that I would be worried. It's like the glittering surface of the water when the sunlight coats the lapping waves with twinkling crosses. A fragment might flicker into view but I never see the whole image. Maybe, like just now, the rail of a skiff, Mum's hands as she shoves the picnic basket under one of the seats. A little water pooling at the lowest point. Dad on the oars with his sleeves rolled up, the hair on his arms. Then gone, and nothing more. How old was I? Six? Seven? Ten? We must have been on our way somewhere, but I don't recall. Just the boat, our little boat. Dad's calm rowing, the scraping noise of the oars against the rail, no creaking oarlocks – they were broken, I think – and then the wooden blades as they sliced through the surface, caught and hauled the boat forward. Towards Storholmen in the middle of the river, perhaps. The spot you could walk to in winter before they started messing with the spillways. Mum insisting on snowshoes, Dad getting Tanja to pull the sledge with the ground pads and ice-fishing rods.

The last time I was down by the river in the summer, wasn't there a tarpaulin along the bank? A little mound of dark green, military green? Maybe the skiff is still down there. If that's the case, no one ever uses it. It must be just lying there, as though hidden away. Glittering sun, lapping waves, my hand hanging down in the water, and I can't stop watching it, because earlier that same summer a child dipping their toes in the water had been bitten by a pike. There were pike in the river, that much I knew. Big prehistoric beasts down there in the seaweed jungle. Mum chuckled at my fear, Dad... what's Dad doing? He's watching a flock of waterfowl take off. Following them with his gaze as though in slow motion, his neck extending as he tracks the birds' wingbeats; we can almost feel them from where we sit, drifting this way and that in the current. Maybe Dad is tired and has stopped rowing, maybe his arms are sore, but he has let go of the oars; they glide slowly over the rail and down into the water. Mum hears the splash, but before she can get to them they have floated out of reach. She looks terrified. Dad is still almost bewitched by the birds, who seem to have flown directly into the sun. I tear my gaze away from the pike, but when I follow his instead the light is so dazzling that I'm blinded. Without oars we're tugged helplessly along by the current. Mum says Dad's name, louder and louder, until at last she's almost screaming. But it's as though he neither hears nor sees, as though he is no longer with us in the boat.

The half-eaten loaf of cinnamon coffee bread is still on the kitchen table. Dad sliced it with a table knife and we have eaten a couple of pieces each. Dropped crumbs, drunk coffee. He looks tired, bags under his eyes. The kitchen is messy, even though he was expecting me. I brought the bread just in case. He fetched an envelope of cash. Two 500-krona notes. I told him it was too much. Wanted to take one of them and hand it to him, was just about to pull it out when something stopped me. I heard Mum's voice in the back of my head. So

I just said thanks. He said happy birthday. The bread wasn't dry after all, despite having been discounted. I found it in a basket next to the checkout with a big red REDUCED sticker that I peeled off. Not sure why.

After coffee I head into the living room to have a look. The same old paintings hang on the walls – nature scenes. Mallards. Geese in formation framed against the sky. A woodpecker like the letter V pasted to the trunk of a birch tree. Precisely the kind of artwork you'd see at a flea market among the coffee sets, old barometers and stacks of flowerpots. The images are exactly what the people around here see when they open their front door. He's got the mallards down by the river, and the geese move in annually, arriving and departing again, that's what they do. The woodpecker lives in the Swiss pine on the neighbour's property.

The brown leather armchair faces the window with its worn armrests and cushion, reclined slightly. The television is a few metres away, on a metal trolley with wheels. There's a bit of dirt on the floor and a few dirty plates on the table. On my way back to the kitchen I notice that all the gardening tools are leaning against the wall in the hallway. The rug underneath them is a muddy mess. He is sitting right where I left him, brushing together a few grains of sugar, pressing his finger against them and popping it into his mouth.

He asks about Mum and I tell him about Roger. Then about the tango lessons. 'She sends her regards,' I tell him. He asks me to return the greeting.

'So, how are things with you?' I ask after a moment.

At first he tells me things are fine. I take a little more bread, although I'm no longer really in the mood for it. Slip a piece out of the plastic wrapper, cutting it carefully so as to avoid slicing through the white cardboard.

'I have a hard time sleeping at night,' he adds eventually. I watch him, chewing.

'I wake up after a while and get out of bed.'

'You're probably drinking too much coffee.'

But that's not it.

'It's that bird,' he says.

He sounds defeated, almost a little ashamed.

'The crane?'

'It's not a crane, I told you.'

'Have you seen it?'

'I know what cranes sound like.'

He can't get back to sleep, he says. Sometimes he's up all night.

'You must be exhausted,' I say. 'I go completely crazy when I can't sleep. You've got to see the doctor and get some sleeping pills or something. Or get some of that all-natural tea. Herbal.'

'Nah,' he says. 'You work, that's different. I just wander around this place.'

He gets up and starts clearing the table, probably regretting that he said anything at all.

'No more than two cups a day,' I say as I leave. 'Promise.'

He nods. Wishes me a happy birthday again at the front door. Although it's autumn the lawn is as smooth as a polished apple. He seems to have stopped clearing underbrush by the river. Over next to the dwarf raspberry bushes I see the shed, its door slightly ajar. Light spills out and I feel an urge to walk over there and have a look. Why not? I mean, he's carried all of the equipment into the house; he must've been making room for something. But he's still standing there watching as I leave, so I resist the impulse and turn the corner instead.

On the way home I make a stop at the off-licence. The woman at the till was cute, congratulated me when she saw my ID. She must've been about twenty, no one I recognized. Then I get back into the car again and try to breathe. The pressure in my chest is so intense that I have to lean over the steering wheel.

'Fuck damn fucking fuck.'

A couple walking by with a wine box look my way, so I sit up and twist my face into something resembling a smile. I turn the key, nothing happens. I'm supposed to meet Mum Monday night, she's busy with something until then, and for some reason that pleased me. She asked me what kind of treat I wanted with the coffee when we confirmed the time over the phone, and I said it didn't matter. Then I called Magnus and he told me to come over to celebrate before heading off for Stage.

It'll be good to go there. It will. I straighten up and start the car. On the floor next to me the cans of beer topple over in the bag.

After a few cheap drinks in Magnus's newly renovated kitchen, which is so clean that you hardly dare touch anything, we end up at a corner table at the club and most of the others are already there. Ola and Amanda, who have been an item since high school. Cutie-Malin, Linnea. And Josef, sadly. Rickard stands next to him, drunk and wisecracking and hitting on a blonde girl from Hertsön.

'When girls start coming here from Luleå it's a fucking bad sign.'

I laugh. The blonde's friend is smaller and looks friendlier. She laughs too, maybe she heard what Magnus said. The music is so loud that it vibrates right through you. The lights swing this way and that and I have a cloudy white drink in front of me on the table. She has something similar and raises it for a toast. I lift mine slightly and nod. Press my lips together again, grind my teeth lightly, but I can't continue looking at her. I think of Dad's bird paintings, how they hang there on the wall in that room – the mallards, the woodpecker. The geese. Another dirty plate on the table, the television on, maybe he has fallen asleep there and will wake up stiff and miserable. The bass rumbles through the table and the electric lights flash against my eyes. The blonde wants to sit next to Ola and her friend ends up next to me. She looks at me apologetically as I make room for her. Presumably I look awkward sitting there, as out of place as a tree stump or a spruce. I'm guessing she'd much rather be in Luleå, at the pre-party that was surely much more fun than this. With the evening's possibilities still wide open. I'm sure they sat in the kitchen with some beers just like us and listened to 90s hits. Spice Girls and 'Mambo No. 5'. 'Freestyler'. She leans towards me and says her name is Eva.

I tell her that's a pretty name. I've never thought about it before but that's a damned pretty name. Clean and clear.

Eva Eva Eva, I repeat to myself. It feels bright.

I tell her my name and that my father chose it, that my mother protested but gave up eventually. I see the mallards' mild gaze in Eva's eyes when she laughs at my forlorn expression. I pretend that it's because of the name, but maybe she sees through me. Regardless of the reason, I'm pleased that she laughs.

'It's my birthday today,' I tell her. 'Twenty-six.'

'Happy birthday,' she shouts over the music.

Happy happy happy.

'I saw you at Stage on Saturday,' says Molly when I get to the break room on Monday.

She worked the overnight shift and I am relieving her. None of the old folk are up yet. Molly is seated, dipping her teabag in and out of a white cup.

'But I was getting ready to leave and you seemed busy with a bunch of other people,' she continues. 'I didn't feel like making my way through the crowd. Did you have fun?'

'It was OK,' I reply. 'You?'

She shrugs and wrings out the rest of the tea by squeezing the bag against a spoon with the string.

'Fucking terrible music,' she says. 'I was so over it. They'd dragged up some idiot from Stockholm, DJ Cute... Did you see her? Made me want to puke. Then this guy comes up to me and asks what I'm waiting for. My friend Madde said "better times". I thought she'd said "better guys", so I was dying. Anyway, he left. But then Klas showed up. Soooo, yeah.'

She flashes me a crooked smile and I nod.

'Hey, by the way, I'm going to uni in the spring. Nursing. Then I can come back here and boss you around.'

'Ha!' I exclaim. 'Maybe I'll go back for nursing too.'

'Then we can boss together.'

'Yup.'

'Although I'll be damned if I'm going to work here for the rest of my life.'

'It can't be much better anywhere else. Or do you want to fuck off to Stockholm and be a DJ?'

'No. But I could be a school nurse or something instead. Hand out ibuprofen and tampons and nag about condoms. Let the bullied kids come in with their made-up symptoms and have a lie-down during break.'

I open the dishwasher and start emptying it. Make a tall pile of plates on the counter then move the whole thing into the cupboard. Stack the glasses in twos. Rattle the cutlery down into the drawer.

'Do you think…' I begin, but I lose momentum.

'Do I think what?' Molly yawns.

'Do you think that there's anyone living here who isn't unhappy?'

'What the hell kind of a question is that?'

I turn to face her.

'Honestly.'

She gets up, swallows the rest of her tea and places the mug in the sink.

'It sounds horrible when you say it like that. Kind of nasty.'

'I don't mean it like that,' I say. 'It's just that… I always think that everyone is unhappy, like my dad, for example. He isn't even seventy. Sixty-two. But when I go and see him it feels like he already thinks everything is over, that it's just autopilot from here on. No point trying new things, travelling, making friends. But he could live to ninety-five. That's longer than my life to this point.'

Molly says nothing.

'Is it better to pretend it's nothing?' I continue. 'Maybe it's just in my head that they're all unhappy. The ones who never have a visitor, don't have anyone, who just sit and watch TV every night even though they don't want to.'

'You watch TV every night,' Molly counters.

'Yeah, I know. But I think it's so damned sad sometimes, that I just watch TV or go out and drink. It's like, that's all my life is right now. I don't have any interest in anything. But at least I know that I'd much rather have things be different. But maybe it's just in my head.'

'Well go back to uni, then, do something else besides watch TV if you don't want to watch TV.'

'Yeah,' I say. 'Exactly.'

At the end of the week I call Dad but he doesn't answer. I sit at home in bed and lazily flip through the channels. My body feels heavy, my feet hang over the edge of the bed. I should go out. Get some air. The blinds hang crookedly over the window like a drooping wing. From time to time someone walks by outside. I see only jackets and legs, no heads. I turn on my computer, pull up the university's home page and scroll through the courses on offer. Mum said it was nice that Molly was going back to university. I'm not sure why I told her; she probably thinks I have a crush on her, because she asked what she looked like and if she was funny. Which university is she going to? Mum had baked a layer cake with fresh strawberries and jam and vanilla cream, just like when I was little, except then she used to decorate it with sweets instead. They would be rock hard from being stored in the fridge, so you had to suck on them for a while to be able to chew them. The strawberries tasted shop-bought, hardly any flavour at all. But the cake was good anyway.

I asked her how the dance lessons were going, if she was learning anything. She seemed a bit distracted, asking questions without really listening to the answers. Eventually I heard myself ask about the boat. Suddenly we were both alert.

'What boat?'

'Our boat,' I replied. 'The one we would take out on the river when I was little.'

She got to her feet and fetched herself a glass of water, paused with her hand on the tap and asked if I wanted any. I shook my head.

'You remember that?' she said, as she sat back down.

'Well, not really. Just that we were out once and he dropped the oars.'

'We were always out in that thing. We used to row over to the little island and picnic there. Aron loved that boat. It was his father's.'

'How did we make it home without oars?'

'Do you remember your grandfather? Well, you were very young when he died. No, there's no way you could remember him, you were only a baby. The whole thing was just awful, when he ended up at Furunäset. Nerves, they called it then. That was shortly before they closed, before everyone was let out. Of course, he was dead by then. We all went to the funeral.'

I nodded. Everything she said was just a vague buzzing sound, the unfocused buzzing of a bee circling its hive.

'But how did we make it home?'

The phone gave a sudden jangle that made Mum jump up so quickly that she bumped into the table. The cake server fell off the platter and red jam dripped down onto the white tablecloth. I could hear from her voice that it was one of her girlfriends. They went to the cinema from time to time, stopping for a coffee at the Opal cafe; maybe one day they'd even take a 'pensioners' coach trip' through America, all together, she'd said. After hanging up she told me that Maj was on her way over to borrow a DVD, so I left.

My mobile beeps and when I check it I see Eva's name on the display. I had forgotten that we'd exchanged numbers – her suggestion. Or was it mine? A text. She has sent me a link to a site that explains the meaning of names and written below it: 'Your name isn't so crazy after all...' followed by a smiley. I tap the link and a web page pops up. 'Originally Cymric: guardian of the universe.' I laugh out loud. 'Not at all pompous...' I reply. And perhaps because I suddenly feel different, having laughed like that, possibly the first time I have laughed in this apartment, I go on to ask if she wants to meet up. She replies, 'Yes.'

Just imagine if the two of us had a baby, I think, sitting opposite Eva in the cafe's outdoor seating area. She is beautiful and glowing, like her name. She could be holding a baby now, her hands around a warm, compact little body. It could be mine and hers, gurgling and smiling and so beautiful that people walking by would smile kindly at us, thinking, 'What a happy little family. Now there's one happy little family.' Mum would be so pleased. And Dad. Maybe they could meet Eva's parents, have dinner. We could walk to the Chinese place – it would be a little formal at first, Dad would've made an effort and ironed his shirt, Mum would look a little worried but still tender, and would make sure that Dad didn't order something he wouldn't like.

Eva and I are at the Opal and she's telling me about her job. She works for a newspaper publisher in Luleå but drove here to meet me. She's wearing a blue trench coat and a touch of lipstick. Everything she says is easy to listen to, sort of gentle. She laughs, I laugh. I talk with her effortlessly. Eva orders cafe latte and I do too, plus a light-green marzipan cake shaped like a frog with an open mouth. It's the one I always wanted as a kid, when we would walk here for a treat, me and Mum and Dad. Such a childish thing to buy, but Eva didn't react to it. They're barely edible, so much buttercream, but that doesn't matter. You don't have to eat the pastry on a coffee date, it's mostly to have something in front of you. It's the kind of thing you do, take a walk and have a coffee date, it's nice. The birch trees on the pedestrianized street are so beautiful that I can't help glancing over at them, sparkling yellow and orange, the high expanse of the autumn sky behind them infinitely blue. My gaze shifts between Eva and the sky. Not many other people out, this sunlit day in the middle of the week.

'This is probably the last day for sitting outside,' Eva says. 'We lucked out with the sunshine,' she adds, and I say that yes, we really did.

Yes yes yes.

Over near the intersection on the other side of the street I see the entrance to the big supermarket, rows of shopping trolleys just outside, glistening in the sunshine. Red handles, coin slots, narrow metal bars. A woman deposits a coin and removes a cart with a yank. It rattles as she steers it towards the entrance, swerving to avoid a pitiful-looking man. As my gaze passes over them I think that the poor fellow looks like he hasn't slept in days. He stands with his back towards me, peering into the sun. As if he was on his way somewhere and then forgot where he was heading. Just ended up standing there. You're probably on your way in to buy groceries, I think for him. You're going to get a little food for the weekend, maybe a few beers, a nice piece of meat and a sauce mix, make it cosy at home, rest a little. Maybe he escaped from a home of some kind and got lost, that sort of thing happens. But he isn't one of mine, I think. Then he turns round and starts searching his pockets slowly, as if creating a distraction so that no one will wonder why he's just standing there, maybe giving himself some time to remember.

Then I see that it's Dad.

My body stiffens and I stifle an urge to leap up and go to him. Eva stops talking and turns to see what I'm looking at.

'It's my dad,' I say.

I immediately regret saying anything, without really know-ing why. It is my dad, after all, he's going shopping, it's Friday afternoon and he's on his way to do a little weekend shop-ping, or for the whole week, since he doesn't go into town that often. The old man who always stands at the entrance selling lottery tickets seems to say something to him, 'Jackpot this Saturday!' maybe.

'Who?' I hear Eva ask as I watch Dad turn towards the old man, drawing his head back so that his neck disappears, like when a bird protects itself from an attack.

But Dad doesn't seem to see the lottery ticket man, his gaze wandering the empty space above him. The man retreats slightly, towards the glass doors. He catches sight of someone else to talk to and turns away from Dad, who is stuck with his head tilted back, scanning the shadowy corner under the awning.

Eva turns back and gives me a slight smile.

'What's his name?' she says. 'What's your dad's name?'

I force myself to look at her, to pretend that nothing's happening even though I know that nothing is, really. After all, it's just Dad on his way to do some shopping, everybody shops, and when you see someone at a distance they always seem a little different when they don't realize that you're looking at them, and besides, Eva hasn't said anything, she's just asked his name.

'Aron,' I answer. 'What about yours?' But I don't hear her reply.

Does your dad go shopping too, Eva, like mine? I think to myself. Do you dream about him at night like I do? Did your dad ever drop the oars when you were little? Do you ever wonder how you made it home? Do you remember your mother? Do you remember her expression when she noticed that the oars had floated too far from the boat? Because the current was deadly, you hardly swam in that river, not there, not since they built the hydroelectric dam and made the deeper currents strange, unpredictable, not since the pike arrived and started growing. Do you remember that your mother tried to reach for them, for the oars, almost fell out of the boat, that you had to hold on to avoid falling into the water yourself, but your father didn't even see that, he didn't notice a thing, just stared at those birds as they flew straight into the sun, despite her shouting at him, shouting his name, your father's name, 'Aron! ARON!'? Or was it your name that she shouted? Your weird Cymric shadow-name? I can't remember, can't remember any of that, it was so strange, but I want so badly to ask, 'Eva, what kind of father do you have, a safe one or a mean one? Or one like mine?'

I realize that I've eaten almost the entire cake. The silver spoon slices through the marzipan, through to the bottom, then angles upward to collect a big piece and puts it in my mouth. The whole time I keep talking to Eva, or rather it's mostly her talking, and soon my plate is scraped bare, empty.

It's time to leave. Eva has to get back to Luleå. We hug by her car. The sunlight is still strong and beautiful. Once she has shut the car door and I've turned round to leave it is suddenly unbearable to think that it's the weekend and I'm going to be alone without anything to do. I should be with her, but she didn't say anything about it. Maybe she already has plans, or has to work; maybe she mentioned it and I didn't hear. Did I hear anything she said, did I respond? Maybe I behaved so badly that she got scared or felt uncomfortable. Did I really eat the whole cake that quickly, bolting it down, without even looking up? Or worse, staring at her the whole time, her speech growing slower and slower, while I got whipped cream and marzipan all over my face?

'Remember when you used to have your sessions with Bengt-Erik, when you were little?' Mum says, replacing the album on the shelf.

We've been looking at old photos – I wanted to see pictures of myself when I was a kid. And of Dad, and that old boat.

'When you and Dad got divorced?'

She hesitates for a moment, but then pushes the album in the rest of the way and comes over to sit next to me on the sofa. She's so happy when I visit her, to have a chance to see me, she said so when I called. At that point I was already standing outside. First I go to Dad's place, then I come here. It's like a song I've always sung.

'No, this wasn't then. This was earlier. Did you know that he's changed jobs now? He doesn't work with children any more, just adults.'

'Hm,' I say. 'So how's the dancing going? Learning anything?'

Mum smiles slightly and shrugs, which is unusual. That's something she doesn't typically do, shrug her shoulders like that.

'Do they still just want to dance the Finnish version? I didn't know there were two kinds, but that's what you said. You've got to tell them that you should all give the other one a try, if that's what you want.'

She lays a hand on my arm and strokes it. The hairs on my arms feel electric. Just as I'm about to ask her to stop she takes her hand away.

'Oh yes,' she says. 'Don't worry. You shouldn't spend your time worrying so much about things.'

'I don't worry that much,' I say, and think of Dad.

After Eva and I had finished our coffee and she headed back to Luleå, I drove out to Dad's place, thinking I'd wait for him there to see how he was doing. But he was already home, in the middle of trimming the bushes at the front of the house, a big pile of twigs on a tarpaulin nearby. Drenched in sweat. The hedge trimmer wasn't great but at least it worked, he said.

He hauled away the tarpaulin and dumped the twigs onto the compost heap. Then I followed him to the back of the house, where he leaned the trimmer against the wall under the overhanging roof and I peered into the darkened corner.

'Why don't you put it in the shed?' I asked. 'What are you up to in there anyway?'

He had been working there too. Said he was going to fix the floor, it was so rotten.

'First I brought everything into the hall so it wouldn't rust to pieces,' he said, 'but it made such a mess that they had to go back outside. Hasn't rained in days anyway.'

There were lots of things lined up against the wall. Rakes, pitchforks, the digging bar he would drive into the ground to make a hole for the maypole. And the spiral ice auger, the light-green paint almost completely flaked off. Dad saw me eyeing it. In my head I could clearly hear the sound it makes as you turn the crank and work it through the ice. First the surface snow, with a slight crunch, no resistance, then the deepening sound as it bites into the harder layers. You're supposed to hold it completely straight, then once you've got it well into the ice you just crank away. When it punches through you've got to hold on: it tries to get away from you, but you have to pull it back up so that the crushed ice drops out onto the snow, uncovering a round black hole down into the deep. Down to that other place, cold, to the undertow with its many hooks. If you stick your arm down into the hole you can imagine one of the currents reaching up to meet your hand, grabbing hold and hauling you down until your shoulder collides with the ice so hard that it splinters, then it yanks again and you're drawn through. And then you find yourself down below.

Below below below.

But even if you are afraid, that fear is also like a wave of light inside you.

I felt such an urge to touch the auger, hold it in my hand. Hear that wonderful sound again, as it passed through the ice. As it found its way down. I tingled, like when you're young and you see some large creature at a distance, like that time Dad pointed through the windscreen at an elk running on the wrong side of the game fence, looking for a way back in. Dad drove slowly alongside it, because at any point it could throw itself onto the road and right at the windscreen, cracking it, and crash through. There was fear in the elk's eyes, the whites visible around the dark edges. That's how it felt to imagine the sound of the auger, like the elk's frightened eyes. Like the pike. I took a few steps towards the wall and the auger, but Dad stepped in front of it and asked whether we shouldn't have a little coffee. It was like he was saying it for my sake.

'Let's go in and have a cup,' he said. 'My hands are so tired from the trimmer.'

And I followed him into the house. The sound of the auger carving through the ice faded from my mind.

'That's right, you were obsessed with walking out on the ice and drilling holes,' Mum says, and I am suddenly confused because I can't tell the difference between what I've said to her and what I've only been thinking.

I'm not getting enough sleep, I think.

'You went out at night that winter,' she says.

'Which winter?'

'When you started talking about pike. You remember that, don't you?'

I say nothing.

'But if you feel that worry coming on,' she continues, 'you can just talk it through. It doesn't have to be with me, you can go to Bengt-Erik. You've known him for ever.'

She smiles her serious smile, lips pressed lightly together and eyes wide open like a goat or cow. She looks ugly. Prim and proper.

'You've always sought clarity in darker waters, haven't you?' she says, once again laying her hand on my arm. *Just like your father.*

I stand up from the sofa abruptly, spreading the fingers of both hands.

'Mum, what are you talking about? Dad's the one who has me worried, and that bird he goes on about that keeps him awake. Do you know he hasn't slept in days? Because there's a bird down by the river that keeps shrieking. He seems lonely and I'm worried about him, that's all.'

'You don't have to keep worrying about Dad,' she says slowly. 'He had problems with his sleep before, during one of his darker periods, but not any more. Now he's on medication, of course. Is it you who isn't sleeping? Are you drinking too much coffee? Two cups a day, max, that's what we agreed. Caffeine will just make you even more unsettled. It's better if you drink that all-natural tea. Herbal.'

I just stare at her. Tell her I have to go, I have shopping to do.

'You go ahead, do your shopping,' Mum says, and gives me a hug. 'Get a good rest. Aren't you working all next week?'

I flow down the stairs like leaking water.

But I don't go shopping. Instead I drive home and try to sleep, unsuccessfully. There's a ticking in my head. Not like a clock, more like something big that's going to burst, maybe not for a thousand years, slowly being prised apart. *Tick tick tick*.

The night floats like a heavy, shapeless mass above my head, as it always does. An oily black horde. I try to force it higher up, prise it off me, so that I won't suffocate. But it just slowly descends towards me. I am helpless in its presence. Now and then something darts out of the mass, down towards my face, and strikes me. A thought? An image? Something I've said or done? A movement, a glance? It can be just about anything that lunges out at me. One of the black pike from my childhood that's grown large. Its pointed snout thrusting at my eyes or cheeks, temples. I can't stop it, can't do a thing. It strikes, I twitch, without losing my grip on the shapeless night. If I did it would all tumble back down and suffocate me immediately. Plug my mouth, slide in through my nose, twist itself around my neck and start squeezing, strangling. All this has already happened, I think, right here where I'm lying. Now it's my turn. I see before me Dad lying in his bed, just like me, unable to sleep, listening to anything ticking or knocking or flickering in the deep.

It's nights like these when you get up. Eventually you hear something, a bird calling, a noise you've never heard before, the sound of something magical. From a secret other world hidden behind this one. You feel relieved and go outside, thinking, 'Finally!' Finally it has come. The bird that never comes. It has come to fetch me at last.

And these endless, lonely nights,

This pitiful little life, wasn't everything.

I follow Dad's meandering tracks into the dream. There is the shed, in the darkness on the point. The river a dark expanse behind it. The door unlocked, he's in there. My fingers approach the handle. With a jerk, it's open. In the middle of the workbench Dad has built something out of twigs, something round and gigantic, under a swaying copper-coloured heat lamp. He hunches over as he moves, bowing towards the golden oval that lies in the middle of the twig nest, glowing amid wandering shadows.

It's glowing, glowing.

'Do you hear its wings beating out there?' Dad whispers. 'Like thunder.'

My knees buckle, striking the wooden floor so hard that I whimper. Dad comes towards me with his eyes like two golden ovals of light, sinks down near me with sweaty, nervous fingers. We kneel together before the nest, Dad and I. Inside the translucent shell I notice a sudden movement. The hatchling emerging. With every jolt something shudders in me. In my body of flesh and dust and steam. Within me, someone larger stomps in their stall. Crowded, as if I might burst. 'Come out,' I say. 'Fight your way out.' My face pressed against my father's, he smiles at me until I also smile, and we grow larger and larger, maybe he laughs, or maybe it's me, his face is so close to mine, until all I see is his golden gaze and smiling mouth. And then the sound of something splintering, and my laughter, a crack forms in the shell, and something clambers out of the egg.

The bird emerges. It opens its beak to call.

After we've descended the slope through the sea of fading lupins and reached the riverbank I see it straight away. Dad steps forward and bends down to get a grip on the corner of the tarpaulin. A pool of water with a few rust-coloured pine needles in it empties down the sides as he lifts it. The boat is lying belly-up, looks just like I remember it. White, blotchy, with a light-green stripe below the rail.

'Can we take her out on the water?' I ask. 'The boat, I mean.'

Dad gestures to the far side of the hull, and then I see the large hole in the bottom. My hands relax. I realize they've been clenched the whole time.

'When did that happen?'

'When they picked us up,' Dad replies. 'The emergency services. They must've really screwed up.'

He replaces a few rotten planks of wood that have fallen from the nearby junk pile.

'Although I don't remember a thing,' he continues. 'You don't either, do you?'

He glances at me when he thinks I'm not looking. Then he starts covering up the boat again.

I just stand there and watch, the river's crosses of sunlight sparkling in my eyes as Dad pulls down the tarpaulin, replacing the two heavy stones so it won't blow away. The boat rests underneath, hidden once again. The boat we had started to row, but then drifted around in, lost, once the oars were gone. For all these years it's been lying there, ever since that last time. When Dad left us without leaving, once he'd seen the birds. I remember it now, but I can't say anything to him about it. I don't remember everything. Just a little. The way the boat was hauled along with the current. Mum's screams, Dad's oddly glazed stare. How he didn't understand the danger, just kept saying that we were moving in the wrong direction. That we needed to follow them. Mum asked what he meant, what he was talking about. She started shouting for help. Knew that we were approaching the dam. But we never got that far. A neighbour alerted the emergency services and we were rescued. Spared. A red and yellow boat bore down on us from upstream. Our boat bumped into theirs so hard that I fell over. That I remember. Must've been what made the hole. Then we were offered yellow thermal blankets, which Dad refused, saying, 'What's this nonsense?' Dad kept talking, but no one understood any of it. Mum wept. And when we reached land Dad went along with them to the hospital. He didn't want to, but did it anyway. Then he was gone, I don't know for how long. That's all I remember. That, just like his own father, Dad went away. Maybe I'll go away too, one day. Maybe all the way to one of the poles, following the whales through arch after arch, or down into some murky pond where everything is lonely and withered.

Or I'll get to stay here.

On the way back up to the house I ask how things are going with the bird. If he still hears it calling.

He hesitates before answering.

'It happens,' he says eventually.

'And you still don't know what it is?'

'Nope.'

We've reached the veranda. He's wearing his old wind-cheater, the one he's had for ever, and behind him the river glitters like gold. Above us a passing line of geese heads southward.

'Although with time you come to feel like you know anyway,' he says.

I nod slowly. Wanting to say something more, about all of it, but somehow the words just won't come.

The Cat

A cat lay in the ditch along the turn-off towards Skogså. It
was one of those long, strange autumn days, after I'd started
Year 8 but spent most of my time trying to learn about magic,
if supernatural powers existed and if so, which ones. As we
approached in our car I saw it lying stretched out on its side,
eyes shut, right at that lonely boundary of country road,
forest on one side and rubbish dump on the other. It looked
like it was sleeping, right up against the thicket that rose up
behind the filthy yellow shipping containers. A thick river of
greenish sludge oozed along the bottom of the ditch, stud-
ded here and there with glistening shards of glass from the
large bell-shaped COLOURED GLASS container a bit further
away. I saw the cat first, but didn't even have to say anything
to Mum. I had just had time to register it and then she saw
it too. Mum told Dad to stop the car, and once he'd pulled
over she and I both stepped out under the restless clouds that
arched above our heads. I hoped that it was dead. This was a

ninety-kilometre-per-hour road; most died immediately. You saw them along the hard shoulder on your way into town. Mainly squirrels and foxes. Rabbits, birds. Once a badger, striped and handsome like some kind of extraterrestrial. Some managed to make their way a bit deeper into the undergrowth and got to die in peace. But all of them died.

As we came a bit closer we could see blood trickling from one ear. A thin, bright-red rivulet that had already begun to dry up. Both Mum and I recognized her. It was the stray. She had no name, but her coat was a brindle of black and brilliant silver. Often she was swollen, or had a kitten at her heels. But now she was little and empty, her ribs visible through her fur.

The cat had been left to roam free after her owner returned to the city a few years earlier. One of the summer visitors, the kind who came and went from their cabin facing the marsh, probably thought it would be fun to have a kitten while on holiday, something to entertain the children. Figured it would survive, and left. That's what Mum had said. Someone in the village had tried to take the cat home with them, after seeing it wandering around without a collar. Winters wouldn't stop coming, after all. Others had got involved. Mum would probably have taken it in, if only Dad wasn't so allergic. But it was as though the cat had become feral the instant she wasn't around humans any more. No one managed to catch her. For two winters the cat had survived on her own, almost miraculously. And it wasn't winter that eventually took her, it was the road.

But the cat wasn't dead. When we were just a few steps away she opened her eyes. One of her eyelids lagged behind the other. But the whites of her eyes flashed; that was the fear.

She tried to crawl away but her hind legs just dragged along the ground. I stopped, could hardly even look at her trying to escape us. What could I do? Nothing. The cat could be dangerous too, after all, clawing and biting. But Mum was at her side in an instant. She let out a strangled sound that made my body grind to a halt, as if all the fluid had been wrung out, leaving behind only a crowded mass of shrivelled husks.

'Come on!' Jimmy shouted from the back seat, knocking on the window with his hockey stick.

Mum didn't seem to hear. She squatted down and laid her hand on the cat, so lightly that she barely made contact. It seemed to relax slightly, or maybe it was too weak to react any more. Its lower back sloped oddly. The increasing drizzle prompted Dad to turn on the windscreen wipers behind us. Mum shook her head slowly, no longer looking quite so large herself, watching the cat.

Jimmy knocked on the window again. He was late for practice, that's why he was carrying on. The sludge in the ditch smelled acrid and toxic. Probably seeped out of all the metal and plastic caught behind the grate up the hill. The greenest shade had collected in a viscous streak on the surface of the mud. Not a single blade of grass grew on the whole slope, everything was dead. Just gravel and earth and poison.

'Her back's broken,' Mum said.

The cat's eyes had drifted closed again. Her breathing was weak, almost undetectable. Her tail was caked in mud. Mum looked round, her face completely calm, like at home when she was trying to remember where she'd left the newspaper and methodically excluded various alternatives. Off to the right, just behind her, a rough grey stone lay half buried in the hard, compacted gravel. Her fingertips whitened as she started wiggling it back and forth until the earth relaxed its grip. The rain dripped from her fingers and forehead as she raised her hand. It went so quickly, the first blow; I turned away but still saw. Stone against fur. Stone against flesh and bone.

She removed her jacket, wrapped it round the cat and lifted her up. On our way back to the car I saw Jimmy roll his eyes in the back seat and point at his watch. Dad opened the window.

'Not in the car!' he yelled.

She hesitated, just for an instant, and then turned towards me. Maybe it had already happened by then, the change, because I remember that her eyes were ablaze with – something.

'Will you open the boot?'

On the same day that she and I buried the cat under the old willow tree, Mum moved up to the attic. Everything happened so suddenly, no one had a clue where she was. I went out and searched the garden. When I came back in later, Jimmy told me where she'd gone and that the door was locked. She had taken several things with her: the camp bed, the little armchair from the living room, several of my books that were actually hers. From time to time she came down to eat, otherwise we hardly saw her. Aside from hockey, Jimmy was still grounded and he mostly stayed in his room. The house turned quiet. Dad didn't say a word. Not at first. I heard him mention it on the phone to one of his friends and laugh, but there was something new in his voice, something nervous, as though there was a little creature with sodden fur in his throat that he couldn't swallow.

We waited for her to make one of her famous 'pronounce-ments'. Mum was an old hippy, after all. Or that's what Dad used to say. 'One week it's the government, the next we can't eat meat and then it's some war she's read about in the news-paper.' I knew the stuff he said about Mum was mostly in jest, because he usually liked her ideas. As long as he didn't have to do anything, like join a protest, make a list, staple information to billboards or stand outside the off-licence collecting money to save the old railway bridge that no one used any more. But she wasn't anywhere near as flighty about these causes as Dad made her out to be. Mum had always been political. In the past her pronouncements had arrived a bit unexpectedly and could be pretty fiery. When my brother and I were younger we mostly listened, absorbing her words with varying degrees of interest, but lately he and Dad had formed a united front and started talking back. Sometimes this led to fights. My brother would chuckle at Mum when she got fired up and that made her absolutely livid. Dad loved it. I usually wouldn't say much. For the most part I agreed with Mum, but if I let on, both Dad and Jimmy would tease me mercilessly. So I kept quiet.

From time to time she would weep for a whole day about something she'd read. Like the war, most recently. She had pleaded with Dad for us to foster one of the refugee children. But he said no, that we didn't have space. Or time. And that Mum worked all the time; him too. She went on and on – no one could nag like her. Then someone called from the police station about Jimmy and and after that she didn't nag about anything at all. All of her energy was redirected towards talk-ing to Jimmy. She would go into his room and close the door and stay in there for a long time. Then she wanted Dad to go in there too, but he claimed she was much better at that kind of thing. They started arguing, mostly her. 'Don't you get it?' she screamed one night. The sound passed right through my door and deep into my body. 'Don't you get what they've done?' But then she stopped screaming. Stopped arguing too.

She had grown so quiet that everything turned strange, and then she left me behind down there in the strangeness, went up to the attic and locked herself in.

After Mum moved upstairs it became Dad's job to take care of the household, and he didn't shoulder that responsibility silently. He needed recipes for even the simplest meals and he complained that Jimmy and I never helped out, that he was like a servant in his own home and that we were the most spoiled children in the world. Jimmy was just as skilled as Mum at slinking out of the kitchen, and consequently I ended up doing everything. I tried to protest but Dad had always indulged Jimmy. 'Let him rest a little, he just got home from practice,' Dad might say if I pointed at the stacks of dirty dishes. And I didn't feel up to nagging, I wasn't like her. But every time I conceded it felt like I lost something, like something ran through my hands and down the drain with the dishwater, like something was extracted from my body and poisoned the ground.

When Mum didn't give up after more than a week Dad started to lose patience. Made trips to the attic in search of things that weren't even up there. He would knock until Mum asked what he wanted, and when she offered to come down with the things he was looking for if she found them, he grew even more irritated.

'Open the door, Ingrid,' he said. 'You're acting like a child.'

But she refused, so he would keep knocking for several minutes. You could hear it through the whole house. I couldn't concentrate on my maths. But she didn't seem to care. Eventually he gave up and came back downstairs swearing, went to the cupboard and rooted around unsuccessfully for a spare key.

When he caught sight of me standing in the doorway he promptly closed the cupboard.

'Don't look at me like that,' he said. '*None* of all this is my fault.'

Then he left. The gunfire from Jimmy's video game was the only sound remaining.

It turned out that she had resigned from her job at the hospital. I was the first one to notice. It was in October and a water leak had forced the headmaster to close the school for the day, so I went home to study. Most of my class had taken off for the cafe they frequented after school or when we had a free period. I wasn't a coffee drinker anyway. When I skipped Year 6 and joined my new class I didn't really have anyone to spend time with; during break I mostly sat and stared at my pen and tried to move it with my mind. That's how it was. Now, after more than a year, I'd got used to it.

On my way home I saw that Klara was back. She was walking into the entrance hall with her friends, coming from the Year 10 corridor. Despite passing within a few metres of me she didn't say a word. She'd been to our house twice.

Her head was shaved. Madde in 10A stared at me darkly. Apparently she was the one who'd found Klara, upstairs in Danne's parents' bedroom. Her dress over her head, smashed. They even pumped her stomach. I thought that it must feel like being turned inside out, twisted, emptied, distorted. Like an old sweater.

Mum must've heard the bang as all my school books landed on the hallway floor, because she came out from the kitchen. It was a pretty comical sight. She had a strip of some kind of meat hanging from her mouth (which was strange for a vegetarian) and looked a bit guilty. Maybe because I'd caught her at large in the house.

'You're early,' was all she said, chewing.

'There's a water leak at school,' I explained. 'Why aren't you at work?'

And that's when I learned that she'd quit.

It wasn't the same downstairs without her. Dad was having some sort of allergic reaction and was whinier than normal, moping around the house, sniffing and rubbing his eyes. Otherwise he just watched TV. Before, she used to come into my room in the evenings when I was doing my homework, stroke my hair and ask if I wanted a little evening snack. Say, 'Surely that's enough now. You don't have to be the best at everything.' I even missed all the outbursts she used to have about things that Dad dismissed as trivial. Ever since I was little she and I had shared secret jokes, like when we'd push out our lower lips with our tongues, cross our eyes and say, 'Wassamaddawidyoo?' Then we'd laugh like lunatics. Jimmy thought we were super childish, so we'd make sure we did it when his friends were over. She knew how to listen and always said the right things. But more than anything she knew when to be quiet. When it didn't help to say anything, because things were just the way they were, in school or when Dad just wouldn't stop teasing. That's when it was lovely that she actually didn't say anything, just stayed quiet for a moment. After that she usually had a suggestion. It didn't have to be anything special, maybe simply that she needed help with a crossword puzzle.

At night when I lay in my bed unable to sleep I thought about her also lying there, right above my room on the rickety camp bed, and then it was as if something found its way into my body. As if another body entered mine, so large that it stretched my skin, my head, and all my thoughts swarmed around until they became unbearable. But I could barely move because the other body within mine was heavy as lead. And once I finally fell asleep I dreamed the same dream as always. Where I found myself in a black void, crammed into the workings of a huge clock, between its golden cogwheels. I tried to extract myself but my sweaty hands slipped on the metal. And the ticking nearly drove me crazy. I had taught myself a technique to wake up before it was too late. Before I was crushed to death. And then I would stand up, make the sign and utter the necessary word to reveal the truth. Then I walked three circles anticlockwise in order to avoid returning to the same place when I fell back to sleep. I'd read about this in one of Mum's books. Sometimes it worked. Other times I woke up into another dream instead, where my room looked familiar but was different somehow. So similar that I thought it actually was my room and even walked three new circles.

Sometimes the room was empty except for the bed, as if to suggest that there was nowhere else to go, and then I would fall asleep into the first dream, or a new, unfamiliar dream I couldn't remember later. Once I tried to resist the dream space by sitting on the floor in a corner of the room after my three circles, rather than returning to bed to go back to sleep, but when I leaned against the wall it collapsed and I fell and kept on falling. That ended my attempts at rebelling against the second dream space.

Before Mum moved upstairs I had explained all of this to her, and she told me that it was helpful to work through your feelings at night, so that you have less to worry about during the day. In a way, that's how it was. I worried less about the things that I worked through at night, but in their place my dreams gave rise to new things to mull over. Would the dream space ever become so realistic that I might go on living there without noticing? In a parallel world, with a similar mum, a similar brother, a similar school, similar books and similar things to worry about? And, above all, would it be easier?

On Saturday I pulled on my winter jacket and went outside to sit on a garden chair I'd carried from the shed. I placed it in the leaves gathered against the fence and angled it towards the attic window. Then I sat there and glared. The window up there was open and I could hear that she was playing music, her old LPs from the 70s. The record player we normally kept in the living room had disappeared a few days after she'd taken off. She was singing an odd tune, not at all the same as the record, with strange words that I didn't understand. Different sorts of words. As though she was singing in thousands of languages. Maybe she was dancing. She used to do that from time to time when she was cooking, on the rug in the kitchen. With her trouser legs rolled up. I waited for her to notice me sitting down there and call to me to come up. But she never looked out.

Later that day, when we were sitting at the dinner table, a few of Dad's friends came over. Mum disappeared as quickly as usual, after she'd greeted them and kissed Dad on the lips. It was Jörgen, from Dad's old job, plus Olof and Rickard, whom he'd got to know during his basic military training. Just before she climbed the stairs she met my gaze and something sparkled in her eyes, I'm not sure what. I opened my mouth to say something, anything. But nothing came, and then she was gone.

Dad's friends thumped Jimmy on the back and said hello to me as I headed for the dirty dishes. Then they sat down at the kitchen table.

'So it's true,' said Jörgen, 'your wife has got a lover up there in the attic?'

Everyone started laughing and Dad took a glass from the cabinet and laughed along with them, but I saw that his face was completely stiff. Jimmy, who had hung around, answered in his place.

'Yeah, we think she's doing some kind of voodoo up there, or has a mysterious women's club.'

That made them laugh even more, and Jörgen turned to me.

'Well, you at least should be allowed in.'

His face was ruddy and rough as a stone.

'I don't want to be a part of some weird club,' I said.

I was immediately ashamed and regretted my words; it felt almost like they were laughing at Mum. But they didn't hear me anyway.

'Damn, you look terrible,' Rickard said to Dad. 'You catch some sort of virus?'

Dad took a seat at the end of the table.

'It's some kind of allergy,' he replied.

'Maybe you're allergic to doing all the housework,' Jörgen shot back, and everyone cracked up again. Jimmy too.

He sat closest to the window, spinning his mobile on the table with his index finger. Lately I'd barely been able to stand the sight of him, his hands had grown so big and clumsy, two limp flippers, and his face was as rough as a hog's. He must have weighed about eighty kilos – I used to be able to outrun him but now I wouldn't stand a chance. He'd built muscle and his voice was getting lower by the day. Now he sounded like Dad and the rest of them. The other day when he passed me the potatoes his hand grazed mine and it was so sweaty I thought I was going to vomit, turn inside out, and then various images came into my mind of how he looked when he was naked, both when he seemed fully grown and when he was in that gross in-between phase of fuzz and smirks and flakes and pimples. He used to be smooth just like me, but now it was as though he was coated in a thick layer of grease. We used to play together when we were younger, and sometimes had a bath together too; now the mere thought of all that nearly brought me to tears. As if someone was going to force me to bathe with him now, as if he could climb into the bathtub when I was in there without asking, and then what would I do? This heavy, sweaty, meaty machine. He would just smirk at me, like he did at everything, and then twist my arm until it fell off or my skin was torn to shreds.

When I'd finished the washing-up I dried my hands on the tea towel and left the room. My homework was all done, which was a minor miracle. I knew that Dad and his friends would play cards and drink beer all night. Jimmy would presumably play video games as usual. No one would bother me.

I took out my portable CD player and sat on my bed. Soon the whole universe was filled with The Cure and not even the slightest sound from the kitchen could penetrate the music. I stretched out on the bed with my hands on my belly and closed my eyes. Started the yogic breathing Mum had taught me and tried to enter that special, almost meditative state I occasionally found myself in when listening to certain music. Before I even felt tired I'd fallen asleep.

When I awoke the CD had finished. It was after one in the morning. I could hear through the wall that there were still people in the kitchen, even though I knew that Dad had to get up early to take the car to the garage. I needed to pee, so I pulled out my earbuds and set the CD player on the chest of drawers. After I'd peed and brushed my teeth I went to the kitchen to get a glass of water. Everyone was still there, Jimmy too.

'Hey there, you,' said Jörgen as I entered.

They were drunk. I could tell because they were all kind of rounded at the edges and Dad was a little red in the face. The windows were steamed up and the table was covered in empty beer cans. I asked stupidly enough what they were up to, in a perky voice that I didn't recognize. My vision was a little blurry, as if I could see all the particles in the air slowly floating around, in and out of everyone's wet mouths, down to their lungs and then up again and into me.

'We're just sitting here talking about life, little one,' said Jörgen.

'You were supposed to hang up the laundry,' I told Jimmy, but felt ashamed, so proper, just like in school when everyone rolled their eyes as I raised my hand.

Jimmy had a beer in front of him, his hand closed around it.

'I'll get round to it,' he said.

'Jimmy's sitting here soaking up some words of wisdom from those of us who've been around for a while,' said Jörgen.

'A little beer too, I see,' I said before I could stop myself. I took a glass from the cabinet and filled it with water.

'A little beer never hurt anyone,' Dad chipped in. 'He's almost eighteen.'

'He's sixteen,' I said.

'How old are you now?' Jörgen asked, slurring slightly.

'She's thirteen,' said Jimmy.

'Uh-oh, then we'd better watch ourselves,' Jörgen told Olof, prodding him with an elbow.

'You're not a spy for Big Sister up there, are you?' Olof asked.

I started saying that I wasn't anything, but Dad interrupted me.

'As long as she's up there I'm the one who makes the decisions down here,' he said, 'and I don't think a beer or two is anything to nag about.'

'Suit yourself,' I said, and walked out.

They started laughing again.

*

Once back in my room I crept into bed and pulled the blanket up to my chin, but I knew I wouldn't be able to sleep. Couldn't get Jimmy's condescending goddamned expression out of my head. It's the one I pictured on his face when I thought back over everything that had happened, which I didn't even know anything about. The whole school knew more about it than I did, because no one ever told me anything. Not even Mum. Everyone just stared, or looked away. All I had was fragments torn loose. Plus I'd never been in Danne's house, where the party was. Apparently there were often parties there, maybe his parents travelled a lot. But despite never having been to his house, or to any party ever, I could picture the door before me. I could see everything, through time and space. I could see through walls. How the living room is full of beer cans, how the windows are steamed up and there are people standing everywhere. They're making out and shouting to be heard over the music that has burst the speakers, which have started hissing just like Jimmy's speakers do because he's never careful and always does exactly as he pleases. Someone is smoking cigarettes, maybe even indoors. Many are out on the veranda. A blonde girl is vomiting into the hedge and it looks like there are flecks of blood. But I turn my gaze away and force it upward, towards the door on the second floor. Up there everything is quiet. The bedroom door is the one to the right of the stairs, painted white. It's ajar. The music from below is muffled and sounds dull and groaning, as if it's being played backwards. The light from the hallway falls across the darkened room, the bed is made, but the bedspread is rumpled and has been pulled away from the pillows. And there lies Klara. Sleeping, in the middle of the beam of light from the hallway. As if she's gone upstairs to take a nap, to get away from everyone for a moment. Maybe she had a fight with Madde – otherwise they'd be together, just like they always are in school. But Klara has probably got so drunk that she's just gone to sleep. Everyone at school says that Klara loves to party; that she always has to drink until she passes out. Her face is turned away, so I can't see her that well. I can see through all walls except this particular one – here I just peer through the gap in the door, but my gaze loses its way in the darkness on either side of the beam of light. There lies Klara, and her long hair has spilled out across the bed. It disappears in the folds of the bedspread so that it looks like it's super long, reaching down over the edges of the mattress. Klara is the most beautiful of all the girls in the whole school; even when she's passed out she is prettier than everyone, lying there in the light that falls across her from the hallway. But it is so dark in the corners of the room. The darkness swells and shrinks again, but somehow grows and grows. It takes over everything. And then it's as if it all disappears from my view, sort of sinks below my field of vision. The strip of light from the door flickers; someone has walked in front of it. Movement in the darkness. The light is broken again. There is someone else in the room.

Maybe they did it for a laugh, I don't know. I just see a large hand pulling up her dress and then I see nothing else. The flickering light gathers and expands until I need to look away and then the whole scene disappears. But I know that Jimmy was there. I know it, because in science class I heard

Mikaela explain to Linnea that Madde had told her Klara had said so to the police. Before she retracted her report, she told the police that Jimmy and Danne and Robin and Ante had been in the room. Despite her being so drunk that she'd fallen asleep, she noticed they were there. And maybe she'd seen Jimmy's grin, his idiotic goddamned grin, maybe that's what she'd seen then. The same one he had on his face sitting in the kitchen now, as if nothing had happened. As if nothing at all...

And out there sat Jimmy and Dad and Olof and Jörgen and Rickard, laughing. I could hear it all the way into my room. Maybe Mum heard it too, or maybe she was sleeping. It didn't make much difference any more, since she didn't do anything, just let them go on laughing as they pleased.

After maybe twenty minutes I heard the kitchen chairs scrape on the floor. Soon after, Jörgen and the others passed by on the street outside my window, their voices growing fainter and fainter until they finally faded. And then it was silent for a moment. No one went to the bathroom to brush their teeth – both Dad and Jimmy were still sitting in the kitchen. I saw them when I looked right through the walls: they were having a silent conversation, animated, agitated. But I wasn't able to make out anything they said, I could just see them sitting close together, knocking a couple of beer cans together and draining them of the last drops. A few minutes later the outer door opened and closed. I sat up in bed and turned off the bedside lamp so that I could see out into the darkness. It was Jimmy, on his way to the shed. I saw how the door caught slightly when he pulled on the handle, as it usually does in the winter when the frost heave shifts the threshold. He jerked it open and disappeared inside. After a moment he came out again with something long and thin in his hand. I walked to the window and peered out from behind the curtain but couldn't see what it was. He came back into the house, and I heard him and Dad talking but not what they said. They laughed a little and then one of them shushed the other.

It was quiet again. Then I heard a creaking sound on the staircase. Suddenly I understood. It was the crowbar.

They were going to break into the attic.

I almost ran to the door, felt like I had to stop them. But I didn't. What difference would it make if they broke that door open? They probably just wanted to joke around a bit with Mum. *It's only a joke.*

But an odd light shone within me. And I knew that it wouldn't be enough to shout. To stop them I needed to take the crowbar away from them with my own hands. It was the only way.

So I opened the door and walked out into the hallway. I was about to run up the stairs when I heard a sound like a tortured animal as they prised open the door and shouted something to Mum. I froze mid-stride. There was a sudden, total silence. Something ice-cold ran slowly through my body. I could feel how it snaked down my throat, into my stomach, out of my sides and over my thighs until it gathered within my knees in two swirls. That's when I heard someone crying.

Mum.

The crying intensified, first a shriek and then almost a howl. No, not a howl, it sounded more muffled. It grew louder, so loud that I didn't even hear it when Dad and Jimmy came back down the stairs. They said nothing as they passed me where I still stood, ready to leap. Their eyes looked completely vacant as they disappeared towards their rooms. Mum's weeping moans continued up in the attic, but I stood still, instead of going up to comfort her.

The following day I awoke late, lay in bed for a while and listened. Dust moved in dreamlike patterns above my face. The house was silent. I got up tentatively. The whole place felt so empty. Jimmy's door was open. The bed was unmade.

The attic staircase ascended into darkness, the worn wooden steps smooth under my feet. I walked as quietly as I could; halfway up I could see that the door to the attic was ajar. Obvious damage from the crowbar. Pale-coloured wounds in the wooden door frame. Light streamed out over my feet.

'Mummy?'

I pushed open the door.

It was incredible how much she had been able to tidy it up. I remembered the attic as cluttered, dark and dirty. Overgrown windows, a thick layer of dust on heavy rubbish bags and forgotten furniture. But now it looked like any other room. Smelled faintly of citrus, wood and incense.

From between two dark-purple curtains the mild winter light fell across a desk full of books. In the middle stood a glistening typewriter with a blank sheet of paper. The camp bed was made and on the floor next to it was a half-empty glass of water. A few thin, downy hairs were stuck to the edge of the glass, the water lightly covered in dust. I took a few steps towards it but stopped again. A sound, like a thud. Or a dull tone played from somewhere in the house, muffled by its journey through the walls but reaching me in the exact moment that I stopped. I stood motionless and listened. A magpie's distant chattering outside the window. Nothing more. It was colder up here and I was barefoot on the wooden floor. A few centimetres from my toes I saw that someone had drawn a white chalk line that disappeared under the red Persian rug on the floor in front of me. My hand trembled a little as I hid it behind my back.

I was very close to the edge now – of something.

Very slowly, to avoid being seen, I opened my mouth slightly. The rest of my body was still, this was essential. I made the sign with a quick motion of my hand against my spine, it was barely visible. The concentration made the skin on my face tighten across my forehead and temples. I spoke the word very softly, calmly and peacefully, almost completely in silence. But it was probably audible anyway.

Then I took my first steps in a circle, towards the sun.

When I was finished I stood still again, my whole body numb. My gaze searched the room, but nothing happened. I couldn't even hear the magpie now. I turned to leave. But halfway from the room I caught a billowing movement out of the corner of my eye. Down near the floor, behind the curtain next to the closest window. As if something that had been sitting there for a while was now beginning to emerge.

How Things Come to Seem

She raised her hand to block the evening sun as she watched the train roll in towards the old station house. A few cumulus clouds drifted across the distant blue and two men sat smoking on a bench in the shade on the other side of the tracks. The blades of grass poking up between the rails bent as the black engine glided past. She gripped the handle of the wheeled suitcase that stood beside her on the cracked asphalt and began walking along the platform.

The train had departed from Narvik and travelled down through the mountains to come to a halt here and uncouple the two carriages whose final stop was Luleå. The remainder would journey through the luminous night all the way back to Stockholm. Brakes screeched until the train settled with a sigh. The clock on the dark-brown station building read twenty minutes to ten. The sun was still high in the sky.

It felt strange, she thought, to even consider moving here. It was different for Martin. He had grown up in this community.

Went to school here, fell in love for the first time. Used to sit on the swings in the park with his friends every teenage winter and drink booze because there was nothing else to do. Nowhere else to be.

But now there *was* another place to be. Every other place in the world, in fact. Theoretically they could move to Paris. Or Buenos Aires. Maybe, worst-case scenario, Gothenburg, where they'd met at a conference. But he wasn't interested. He wanted to stay. He had bought a villa in 'like, Hamptjärnmoran'. What a hell of a typical village name. 'You'll just have to give it some thought,' he said, when he kissed her and dropped her off at the station.

She pulled open the heavy door and climbed aboard, leaving the platform empty.

In truth she was probably waiting for some kind of sign. As if she thought deep down that if she could only get home again, set down her suitcase in her apartment, she would know the right thing to do. An intention would come rushing straight towards her. Otherwise she would sit and wait. For an omen. Anything at all. A little rag fluttering in the breeze would suffice, one that dragged itself into the hallway and flopped down in the corner. Or maybe it was already right there in front of her face. Waiting for her to wake up and see.

She carried her luggage down the aisle and found herself in the passenger carriage with its double rows of empty seats. Pushed her suitcase into the empty space behind her seat and laid her little bag on the seat next to her. At the end of the carriage she saw two large rucksacks on the luggage rack that ran along the carriage just overhead. Must be in the dining car. Probably tourists. Flocks of them headed up the mountains in June. A few experienced alpinists went to Sarek. But most were hunting the midnight sun and more easily accessible expanses. They'd disembark in Abisko, with rattling camping stoves and wooden cups hanging from their packs. They came from Japan, Germany, England, China, Korea and the US. France. And Sweden. In July the streams of tourists subsided and the trains emptied. Like now. She slid down into her seat.

More than anything it was the silence she had a problem with. Over time it became unpleasant. She had grown up in Uppsala, right in the middle of town. It wasn't a big city, but it was never quiet. Here there was just a vast density. The density of vastness. The day before, when they had sat on the dock down by the river and stared out at the glittering water, the openness of the place had nearly suffocated her. Martin didn't get any of that, he was used to it. He said the river made him calm. It was the same thing in the forest. In the forest he had spoken unreservedly, about some rock he'd seen or politics or what they were going to eat for dinner. But she had looked around the whole time as if she was going to get jumped. Tried to cover every direction with her ricocheting gaze.

An insight that had slowly grown stronger through the years, both before and after she'd finished her education and got her first job, before and after she'd met Martin, all the years that she'd tried to find her way 'there' – somewhere – was that she hadn't stopped, for a very long time, and seen herself. But only a few days earlier, in the upstairs bathroom in Martin's house (with dust sheets still on the floor, because he was repainting), it had happened. Standing in front of the mirror in the naked light of the fluorescent tube, her hands under the running water, she suddenly caught sight of herself. She had looked at her face, the way it sagged downward from her cheekbones, her nose, narrow mouth, hair, forehead, eyes. And she realized that she always saw the same image of herself in her head, but it wasn't her reflection, not the one she saw before her in the pale light in the bathroom, but rather a snapshot of the instant between when she was sitting on Johan's handlebars (feeling strong and beautiful) and when her expression changed as she floated from the bars (he had braked hard) and in the next instant flew through the air and landed on the asphalt in front of the bike. Eleven, long straggly hair, round cheeks. That intermediate instant, of transition, of happiness/panic. That's what she sees. Perhaps that's also why she often feels like a child in the company of adults, when she has to chat to strangers and there are canapés, champagne.

It never happens that she sees her reflection in a shop window and thinks, 'Ah! That's me!' Instead she arrives at that conclusion by a process of elimination – there's only me here, it must be my reflection. Sometimes, in changing rooms or in lift mirrors, when she sees herself from behind she can recognize her mother, the little slope at the very top of her back, as if she had tried to stand up tall all her life but couldn't manage that last bit. That's as close as she gets – her mother. And when she stood there in front of the mirror, and heard Martin move in the bed on the other side of the wall, she wanted to slowly reach out her fingers towards the glass and touch the surface. Immediately, she imagined, it would make rings, like on the surface of water, and she might be able to reach her hand further in, right into the reflection, feel that there was a space on the other side, then climb up onto the sink and throw herself through it. To behind-one's-self. To in-one's-own-arms. But when she gave it a try her middle finger just met cold glass, unyielding, the tip of her reflected middle finger. She looked up, met her own gaze and had a moment of contact. But no, not even the other recognized her. They both departed, quickly and ashamed, in the same direction, each from her own room.

In the forest it was different. There it wasn't she who saw, but she who was seen. Never before had she faced such surveillance, thousandfold, impossible to comprehend. Her body became strange in its presence, began stretching and twisting this way and that. She tried instead to focus on the patches of sky that were visible above the path they followed, birds darting between treetops like arrows. Ants trying to climb up her shoes and inside her trouser legs. She panicked, so afraid of being bitten that she stomped her feet like a nervous horse whenever Martin wanted to stop and tie his shoelaces or look more closely at some rusty military contraption. He kept finding openings that led underground, or circular fortifications, and then the large spiky blocks laid out in uneven rows to prevent enemy tanks from making their way to the large fort that was apparently hidden further up the mountain somewhere. They were all old ruins, of course. Relics from another time, when people strapped planks to their feet and called them skis.

She was completely uninterested in all that stuff. She watched for wild animals, but quickly determined that she saw more wildlife among the apartment buildings in Uppsala than here. Here they could all hide. And not just deer and lazy rabbits either, like at home. Here there were predators, and elk several metres tall. She'd never seen an elk. Except once at a zoo, but it had just been lying on folded legs chewing a mouthful of nothing. Looked more like a horse or a cow.

But up here there was space for just about anything.

She had talked to Martin about her fear of elk, specifically females. They'd kick you to death if you got too close to their young. Stomped and gored and bit. That's what she'd read. He just said that all elk, even the cows, were shot before they had time to get particularly big. Up here everyone loved to hunt. Everyone but Martin, it seemed. Every other house was decorated with massive elk antlers.

Hunting is for idiots, he thought. Idiots who enjoy caus-ing others to suffer for their own entertainment. 'Arseholes,' he said. She hated that word. It sounded so disgusting. Nevertheless she mouthed it silently to herself without him noticing. *Ar-soles. Arsles.*

In her opinion it wasn't all that strange that people went into the woods to kill, since the forest was so enormous and threatening and constantly did everything it could to reclaim its lost ground. Wanted to squeeze right up through the par-quet flooring, a giant tree teeming with insects. She had seen it trying to break its way through the retaining wall along the back of Martin's garden, spitting seeds onto the lawn. Moss adhered to the brickwork. Slugs gathered on the porch at night, leaving a slippery layer of slime just outside the door. Every night. What were they even doing there? There wasn't anything to eat on the porch. They didn't touch the plants in the garden, just lurked in sticky piles until daybreak made them head back into the vegetation.

This was the place he thought they should live. Right up against all that.

'But what if we have a kid,' she'd blurted out as they carried in groceries from the car. 'How do we prevent the kid from wandering into the woods?'

'Why would we prevent that?' he asked.

This briefly rendered her speechless.

'So that it doesn't get lost and die or get eaten or injure itself or get attacked or whatever the hell,' she replied.

But he just chuckled and said that the kid would learn that stuff early – how to find their way and where to walk and what's dangerous. 'Haven't you read *Ronia, the Robber's Daughter*?'

And as if to prove that everything he'd just said was true, he concluded, 'I survived, after all,' and then smiled slightly in his peculiar way. 'Deep inside, we're all forest walkers,' he said.

She was quiet for a long while, saw before her a slight figure in a white dress walking alone into the deep woods, and heard distant adult voices calling the child's name without it reacting. As if it had become bewitched and could no longer decide for itself. The scene closed with the child drowning in a forest lake, freezing to death or being torn apart by a creature that looked like a blend of wolverine and elk. She said none of this to Martin. He'd never even seen a wolverine despite having lived up here all his life.

The train swayed and there was the metallic sound of a carriage being uncoupled. Through the window she saw that one of the two smokers had got to his feet and was gesticulating excitedly with his arms. The other flicked away his cigarette and looked indifferent. She thought they probably lived in the refugee camp a bit further along. Maybe they were traumatized by war and had ended up in this dump, where there was nothing more to do than sit on a bench, chain-smoke and stare at the trains. Dream about travelling on. About going home, wherever that was.

She remembered a time in Uppsala when she had sat in an ice-cold station waiting for a delayed northbound night train to go and visit Martin. It was early in their relationship, but despite the fact that it was four thirty in the morning and the middle of winter she felt excited and sort of electric. Then an old man came walking slowly along, supported by a smooth cane. Since the departure hall was deserted she had seen him from far away. He was surrounded by a white cloud of exhaled air and wore a flat cap with ear flaps and a pilled black scarf. He approached and sat down next to her, his breathing slightly laboured. Then he nodded his head towards the illuminated platforms visible through the glass doors.

When he couldn't sleep he would come here and watch the trains, he explained. He was a former train engineer; had spent his whole life driving the fully loaded ore trains down from Kiruna.

'Sometimes you wonder how there's anything left up there at all,' he said. 'Stockholm takes everything. Can't be much more than an empty shell left.'

'In Malmberget I think they call it The Pit,' she said. 'The giant crater left over after all that mining.'

She'd read that. He nodded. He asked where she was headed and she told him. His eyes were unusually pale.

'You see a lot in those forests,' he said. 'All those years driving through the darkness, in winter storms and downpours. Fallen trees across the tracks. Trudging through the snow and hacking ice. Everything was black. Except the stars, mind you.'

'Sounds nice,' she said. 'Must've been a lot of wildlife. Elk and such.'

'Sure, elk,' he replied. 'They keep their distance. Just stand there and stare at you from between the tree trunks. But there's more.'

'Like what?' she asked.

'The fog,' he said. 'Hard to see much of anything, thick as milk. And you're lucky that you have the tracks. When it rolls in, it can come to seem, in your mind, as if you should stop and walk out.'

'How do you mean?' she asked, but they were interrupted by a long, shrill note from the PA system and a broken voice announcing that the delayed train was on its way into the station.

'It's like what that Polish poet writes,' he explained, watching her stand up and hurriedly put on her gloves.

'What does he say?'

'It's a she,' he replied. 'And she says, "He walks into the forest" – no, "he walks *up*…"'

'Pretty,' she interjected. 'I have to hurry to the train now. But have a good one!'

He nodded and smiled.

'Have a nice trip.'

She dashed off. Turned round once and saw the old engineer still sitting there, his hands in front of him on the cane, looking out towards the tracks.

*

The train started moving along the outskirts of the little city, over the stream, and past the housing developments, Martin's old high school, a railway yard and decommissioned military installations. The rhythmic sound from the rails increased in tempo as the train accelerated. Then they reached the bridge over the river. After that into the forest. First thin birch, with sunlight flickering through them, which gradually thickened into a mixture of spruce and undergrowth, pines. Then grew coarser, heavier. Darkened. She watched her mirror image in the window. Her eyes looked deep and bright, and in them she saw the dark forest beyond. The upper part of the window was open a few centimetres. A soft breeze coursed in through the gap and stroked her face. It caught a few loose strands of hair, tickling her cheek. She tucked them behind her ears – it had just grown long enough to stay there for a while before falling back across her face. She noticed movement in the windowpane a bit further down, the reflection of the conductor walking through the carriage in his dark-blue uniform. She showed him her ticket.

'Empty today,' she said, and he nodded while jotting something down.

'Are you continuing on after Uppsala?'

She shook her head. He moved along.

She sank back into the seat for a few seconds. Then she opened her little bag to select a book. It was a choice between Torgny Lindgren, Eyvind Johnson and Sara Lidman. 'You know that only one of those authors is from around here,' Martin had said. 'The others are from Västerbotten.' But she didn't care about that, thought she might be able to read her way to an understanding of the place. Read her way to the craving for distance from others, the longing for calm and to sit and stare, and to the small-town racism and homophobia and gun cabinets... *Enough of your dark exaggerations*. She opted for Lindgren.

After a while it grew colder, so she stood up and slid the window shut. She spread her jacket over herself and picked up the book again. The train continued deeper into the forest.

When she awoke the book was lying on the floor. Her neck ached a bit and she slowly sat up. Someone had called to her; the silence following their shout still hung in the air around her. A dream. But it felt so real. It had grown slightly darker outside, night had fallen. She rubbed her eyes and looked around. The train stood still.

Through the window across the aisle she could see a little lake. The dark water was smooth and a bit further out veils of mist swept just above its surface. The tall trunks of the pine trees blended into the dark spruce. Heavy silence. On her side of the train there were only trees, a few metres from the tracks and the sloping gravel embankment. She leaned her forehead against the cold glass and fogged it with her breath, it slowly faded and disappeared. Her head felt large and shapeless. There was a little pressure against her temples as though she was wearing a helmet that fitted too tightly. Her breathing was deep and slow.

But she was awake.

A few moments passed. A wind swept through the carriage, like a draught, even though she couldn't see a single window open. They normally announced why the train had stopped, but maybe that had happened while she was asleep. Maybe it was the conductor's raspy voice over the loudspeakers that had woken her. There wasn't anyone to ask either. She spotted a moth on the other side of the window; it bounced against the glass twice and then vanished into the pale sky. She raised herself halfway up from the seat. The two large rucksacks were gone. The tourists must've got off.

She walked along the aisle and stretched, looked round, and tried to remember which direction led to the dining car. Walked towards the front of the train, past the spot where the rucksacks had lain and beyond into the next carriage. A toilet door was slightly ajar. She entered the sleeping carriage. At the end of it was the conductor's compartment. The door was wide open and the light was on inside. A cone of weak yellow light spilled out across the floor. When she got closer she saw a newspaper lying unfolded on a small table and a uniform jacket draped over the chair beside it. But the compartment was empty. The next carriage was the dining car, dark and locked. Open until eleven. She reached for her mobile phone to check the time, but remembered that it was in her bag. She guessed it was just after one, but what did she know. The nights didn't get any darker than this.

On her way back she stopped outside the conductor's compartment again, lingering. But there was only one route to take; she would meet him, or her, on their return – maybe a new shift had started. She walked back to her carriage. Along the way she tried to peek into the sleeping compartments but the curtains were drawn. She suppressed a sudden impulse to bang on all the doors. Shout for someone. Panic and bash her head against the window until something cracked.

She saw her seat at the far end of the carriage. Had a vision of herself, from outside. As if another version of her stood in the forest, watching herself walking there, back and forth through the empty train. *Eleven years old, the long straggly hair.* It smelled fresh out there, the moss had crept up onto the stones and turned them green. Linnaea flowers and heather grew in the crevices. Her counterpart inside the train had paused, resting her hands on the backs of the seats on either side of the aisle, feeling the coarse blue fabric against her palms. Two rows ahead lay her rumpled bag, collapsed into itself.

She looked out of the window. Behind the translucent mirror image of the train's interior she saw nothing. Not herself out there, just her reflected self standing here in the aisle. Pale face, dark eyes. *The round cheeks.*

She passed her seat and soon she felt the brisk night air flowing towards her. The heavy sliding door at the end of the train was open.

And the forest leaned in towards it, just outside.

Goose pimples spread across her arms in the draught. At the bottom of the steps she saw the gravel. Hard to say if anyone had walked there, it was uneven.

She went out onto the narrow steps. The air didn't seem completely clear; it was as if she couldn't see as far as she'd like. The gravel crunched when she stepped down onto it. She gripped the railing with one hand, as if to reassure herself that the train wouldn't take off without her. That she wouldn't be left there, without her phone.

Should've grabbed my jacket, she thought.

There was a chill in the air but she didn't feel cold. It felt clean in her lungs, the way forest air often does. The trunks of the pine trees looked damp. No birdsong, no insect sounds. Just this stillness between the dark trunks with their coarse, twisted branches. This was an ancient forest. Not that cultivated, monotonous, basic kind that you mostly saw along the tracks. This was something different. From what she'd read, you identified really old pine trees not by their height but by their bark, and the branches, which would have begun growing back upon themselves. For most of their lives they were on their way outward, getting longer, taller. Then came a transition, an insight. Turn back and protect, twist around yourself. They suddenly became so human. Shrunk in height every year that the branches slowly struggled to find their way back towards the body.

She looked in both directions. A bird called out from somewhere, a melodic and pretty song. Three times, then silence again. The train didn't emit a sound, not a creak or anything. As if it had been standing there for a long time, months even. Several years. Become overgrown, let nature force its way in. Let moss cover the roof.

The moon shone overhead, a pale sliver. Shrunken by distance. Her gaze swept across the forest again and then she saw something, practically right in front of her but a bit further in; she focused her vision, blinking to clear the sleep from her eyes.

It was an animal, sitting there. A fox. More grey than red in the dusk, looking right at her. She felt her heart begin to pound. *Lill-Mickel-Gullfot-Rödbyxa* – she murmured the names of foxes from her childhood almost soundlessly to herself. It was perched on a stone, tail hanging to one side. She could see its ears moving slightly.

It was so oddly still. She waved her hand a little, not really sure why, as if it would also move just because she did. It did not. And she didn't want it to approach. Despite its small size it was a wild animal, and she respected wild animals. Since the fox stayed motionless, she felt brave enough to have a look around again. She was suddenly worried that she would miss the conductor if they came walking through the train. But surely she would hear them, it was right behind her after all.

That said, the silence out here was deafening. Drowned out all sound from within. If there was any.

It had made its way into the train as well.

Woken people and got them to walk out. She had slept the deepest, awoken last. Meanwhile, a small crowd of people had gathered outside, maybe even right where she now stood.

The conductor had felt compelled to say something. Point out a bearing.

Someone had yawned. Someone else stretched. A child clutched a toy horse.

The two hikers, a man and a woman, had their rucksacks on. The woman said something to the man and made a sweeping gesture with her arm. Away. They seemed eager to get moving after having sat still for so long. She thought she heard them speaking German.

Her head snapped quickly back to the place where the fox had been sitting. It was no longer there. A shiver ran through her legs and she scanned the ground nearest her, as if the fox was just about to creep over and sink its teeth into her thigh or her foot. She even bent down, got on all fours, and looked under the train. She saw the dark water on the other side. But no fox. No people.

Just the night forest. And her.

She abruptly got to her feet. A sound expanded within her, starting near her stomach, a low wail. Locked within a dark room. It wound its way further up her throat and she opened her mouth. As she inhaled, her whole mouth cooled, and along with the air came something else, the silence. It slid slowly into her and laid itself to rest.

She thought about her luggage, still inside the train. But she didn't need it any more. Her bearing suddenly became clear, like when a pure tone grows stronger and resonates within the body. She descended the stony embankment and the sound of her footsteps was swallowed by the soft moss as she began to walk.

The Father Hole

As Dad's eyelids drop like a guillotine she pulls the car door closed with a click. He turns his gaze towards the road and from her shaded spot in the back seat she can see only his right arm and leg, a bit of his cheek. Dad's sunglasses rest on the dashboard, twinkling at Kore like black stars. The air conditioning rumbles softly. Everything smells new.

As he backs out of the driveway she turns towards the window in time to wave to her mother standing on the flagstones down by the house, watching them leave. The car pauses, a new gear is selected. Then they're off.

Five weeks, they've told her.

It's the same thing every summer. The time is broken into two large blocks and the first has already vanished. Now it's the middle of July and it has grown darker. You can see it in the corners of things, in the crowns of the trees, and the way the lawn has deepened in colour, exchanging its June attire for a duller, dark-green shag.

Five weeks. Kore sinks back into the seat and tries to loosen the belt, but it catches. The midsummer flowers along the roadside have finished blooming, leaving only bare stalks. They were pink, white, violet. When she and her mother decorated the maypole there were too many to count. They picked armfuls of them and that night they stayed up super late, until half past one.

The car slows a bit as they crest the hill. There is only the dry sound of the indicator. Then they turn onto the main road. As the speedometer sweeps past seventy Dad presses a button that locks all the doors.

The departure date had approached like a sudden crest in the road, the far side unknown yet still somehow familiar. Once the day arrived she watched the clock tick away the hours until she caught sight of the car up there along the road. He never needed to call her. She came anyway, as if drawn towards a dark magnet, although her feet barely moved. All morning she had wandered from room to room with her rucksack open. But it made little difference what she packed, everything was already there at her father's place. A new toothbrush instead of the worn-out one she had at home, pink rainwear instead of the green set hanging on a hook in the hallway, countless comic books in the chest of drawers. Toys. Drawing paper. Even small tubes of oil paint that she'd got for Christmas. Everything one could imagine needing was to be found at her dad's place, everything.

And at the same time, nothing.

He was always late and she always sat waiting in the hallway, her hands clutching the handle of her bag. Katja was in the kitchen preparing dinner. Susanna was coming over later and they were going to sit on the porch behind the house, light a mosquito coil, drink wine and talk nonsense. Kore felt a hollowness in her body thinking about it, how everything would go on as usual here. Except her. If she hadn't been waiting for Dad she would at this very moment be taking out the craft box and setting it on the kitchen table, listening to cassette tapes while making a little something out of cotton balls, glue and sequins. And later she and Mum would watch *Disney Hour* and drink fizzy drinks and then it would be *Fort Boyard*. But only if Mum had managed to finish cleaning up, otherwise she'd do that first.

'I wonder if you'll find any snails this year,' Katja said as she took a packet of prawns from the freezer. 'And you've hardly had time to ride that nice new bike. I bet the chain on that one won't jam at all.'

Kore nodded and adjusted her grip on the handle of the rucksack. The wind swept softly through the rowans up along the road. Still no car. The hallway was gloomy.

On the wall opposite the front door were three faded chalk lines that Kore had made when she was three. Mum had eventually got round to finding a leftover piece of matching wallpaper in the attic to cover it, but no more than a few days went by before Kore had drawn a new smudgy picture in black and red chalk in exactly the same place. 'Apparently there was *meant* to be a drawing there,' Katja used to say with a laugh.

The rustling in the kitchen had stopped. When she turned in its direction she saw Katja look away and resume poking at a knot in a plastic bag. Kore peered outside again and then she saw the car approaching. It appeared out of nowhere. She jumped to her feet and slipped the rucksack over her shoulders.

'Call if you need anything,' her mum said, hugging her. 'My little nugget.'

'Have fun now,' she said. 'Havefunavefunafun.'

'Kore,' her father says.

He looks at her in the rear-view mirror. Far behind them the house is already out of sight.

'We're heading to the toy shop,' he says, 'and you can pick out absolutely anything you want.'

The cool breeze through the car brings goose pimples to her legs, from just above her tennis shoes all the way up to the patterned bike shorts. Her thighs stick to the cream-coloured leather seats. She's a little cold but says nothing. Her voice has crept deep inside her, hidden away like a dried pea somewhere in her body.

Dad speeds through an ever-changing landscape, the car moving almost soundlessly at 120. He glances back over his shoulder each time he glides past another car. The tip of Kore's nose happens to graze the window and she wipes it quickly with her sleeve so that it won't leave a mark. Just outside she sees the invisible animals, the seven who have been with her ever since she was little, following along at the side of the road: Titus, Babel, Bollo Sé, Mitko, Masha, Ivrahim and the Long-fingered One. Titus runs ahead, so beautiful. His pearly black eyes shining. The others struggle to keep up, making their way around stumps, through clusters of trees and over the ditch. Mitko takes flight intermittently, it's easier. Ivrahim keeps his distance from the rest. Once they pass the cultivated fields on both sides, all that remains is thousands of metres of game fence. And behind it the forest and its deep undergrowth. She knows that there are other, larger creatures among the trees. They haven't yet revealed themselves, but they are in there.

The road dips down, the sun flickering between the trees. She spots a house here and there, fewer as it gets steeper. Then the world is desolate and empty. They pass an unmanned petrol station, a collapsing barn, a few bare tree trunks facing the surrounding burnt grass. Everything appears to be falling, an empty gaping into nothingness. Then the car arrives at the muddy floor of the valley, rounds a bend and the city spreads itself out before them. A roundabout with a large metal statue in the middle and behind it the smokestacks shooting straight up into thick cloud cover. Steam billows from the storm drains. Outside the bus station a teenager slumps against a railing.

A moment later the car comes to a stop. Her dad exits in a single stride. Kore climbs out onto the pavement and follows him towards the shop. From the corner of her eye she sees that the animals have crept in to hide behind one of the rear tyres.

When they come back out of the shop Kore is holding a thin paper bag containing the doll. A light-blue dress with rustling frills. There were so many to choose from, in the end she just grabbed one. Her hands look grimy in the faint light.

The animals follow her into the car this time, crowding in around her feet on the floor mat. From here on they are in her father's land, living under her father's laws. Their eyes scan restlessly.

*

Among the villas out on Ektjärn everything is calm and still, the sunlight soft as a tongue running over the rooftops. No one is out mowing the grass, the trampolines are abandoned. A reddish-brown cat sits on the bridge outside one of the houses and washes itself. It hesitates mid-movement as they drive by. Kore sees the car reflected in each window they pass. A polished oval stone. And in the centre of the stone, her face.

Once Dad has parked and brought her inside, he directs her to the armchair in the living room. Then he fetches the presents. She receives one after another until her lap is full of small figurines and boxes within boxes and hair accessories and colourful bracelets. These things come from all over the world – her father travels a lot for work, to conferences and institutes. He visits places where people speak like birds, have gold teeth and gaping mouths. He has been to New York, Singapore and Madrid. Istanbul and Lima, once to Sydney. She holds a little lacquered box to her nose and smells the scent of the other life that Dad lives, when she isn't there.

Kore thanks him and thanks him, receives yet more gifts and then, when she can barely hold on to more, he pauses and fishes out a slender piece of jewellery from a red box in his jacket pocket and lays it shimmering across his hand. Hanging from the very bottom of the necklace is a little silver heart.

'This is really more of a grown-up present,' he says. 'But I want you to have it, my little queen.'

Kore eyes the necklace, which seems to flow and ripple even though it's completely still in her father's hands. As he slips it around her neck she hears his voice behind her.

'When I bought this the jeweller said, "Whoever you give that to, you'll have her heart for ever."'

He laughs softly. The light from the living-room lamp makes her dizzy, the little electric filaments flow out into the room and droop towards her. Directly at her dark, yearning pupils.

'Will you promise me that, Kore?'

The voice seems more and more distant, as though it's hovering somewhere above her. 'That you're mine for ever.' She moves her lips but no sound emerges. She wants to say no but cannot; it sounds almost like he's crying now, and the points of light from the lamp slip into her eyes one by one, drawn towards the earth and her face. She can feel the black clump in her stomach grinding, digging itself deeper into the flesh. On her second try her response is audible, but no stronger than a whisper. A final sentence before her voice collapses into itself.

Yes.

At Dad's place her room is in the basement, under the stairs. At night they creak as though someone is walking on them. Sometimes there really is, when Dad is heading to his office. It's at the end of the hallway; she doesn't go there but keeps to the other side. Her room here is bigger than the one at home, light blue and purple. She got to choose the wallpaper herself. The floor is covered with a soft carpet so that she won't be cold. The windows are boarded up. Otherwise the snow might break them in the winter, Dad says. But she knows that it's to keep her from escaping.

If she only had a sister, she thinks, everything would be different. In the adjoining room. A sister, like Snow White has her Rose Red, who dares to raise her hand against all attackers and shout, 'Halt!' They could read stories to each other when they had trouble sleeping, tap messages on the wall in secret code. And her sister could help with Dad, so that he wouldn't get so sad.

The first evening after they've wished each other good-night, Kore lies with the covers pulled up to her chin and looks at the posters he's put up. A violet galaxy on one, two baby rabbits on the other. Between them, a portrait of herself. Dad says it looks just like her, but when she looks at it she sees only a featureless little clump where her face should be. A glowing black stone.

Kore. Daddy's little queen.

The next morning Dad is happy. He sits at the kitchen table and reads the paper with her next to him. The smell of coffee is in the air. The radio is playing Swedish *Top Hits* and Kore draws picture after picture, all of them for him, full of suns and animals and their habitats. Then they play cards, a grown-up game.

'You come from a long line of poker players,' he says, and lays down three of a kind. 'My dad taught me when I was six.'

He likes to teach her things and she listens very carefully and nods the whole time. Her face beams and she can't stop herself from fooling around after a while, trying to get him to laugh by hiding cards up her sleeve, and it works because he smiles and says that she's a card shark just like his cousin Robert, who bought his house with money he'd won at card games.

'He's very clever, that one,' says her dad.

Dad likes it when people are good at doing maths in their head, so he quizzes her on multiplication tables, and she's practised them so much at school that she knows them by heart, even the hardest sum, which Dad says is eight times seven. But then she happens to knock over a glass, watching in slow motion as it rolls off the edge of the table and falls to the floor. Three big shards and lots of tiny ones scatter everywhere. She freezes. He gets up and fetches the broom and dustpan from the cupboard. He says that he isn't cross, but she knows they won't play any more.

They eat lunch in growing silence. The bigger it gets, the harder it is to break. She forgets to chew, just sits there with her fork in her hand. In her leaden mouth her tongue is a fat slug that won't budge. Then she spots the photo of the dogs on the wall behind him, next to the barometer. She says, 'What were your dogs called again, Dad?' – asking although she already knows. Zeus and Argos, and later he had Medea, who died before she turned five. He points to the photo and shows her Zeus, who wouldn't obey anyone other than him, a rare black breed, clever and loyal, though he died long ago. Argos was great too, but none of them were like Zeus.

'He never disappointed me,' said Dad. 'Not even when we came across fresh bear tracks on Porsön and he was petrified. He didn't bolt, although his whole body trembled.'

Kore immediately asks about bears, then about trembling and frothing at the mouth.

After they've eaten, Dad shows her how to build a fire in the big fireplace in the basement. First he tears strips from yesterday's paper, then he lays the thinnest kindling he can find in a square, stacking the pieces on top of each other with room for air to circulate. Then he lights it.

Now it's as though everything that happened earlier is forgotten, because Dad loves fire. He loves to blow on it, to watch the flames eat their way into the wood, to hear the logs whine and to see the black smoke that appears when something living catches fire. He loves to hold his hands so close that they almost catch fire too. But Dad never burns himself. He'll poke a burning log or pass his finger through a candle flame as though he were immortal.

At times like this it can happen that he takes her along with him out of the house. 'This is my daughter, she has finally arrived,' he says to all the neighbours they meet. 'Look how lovely she is. Look at her eyes, so like mine.'

At other times she can tell even before entering the kitchen in the morning that it – something – has happened again. The little animals sense it too. Titus's ears are alert and he assumes a concerned expression; the others press themselves against her legs, seeking protection against the unknown that might at any moment wheel around with a predator's face and a mouth full of teeth. Just seeing him from behind is enough: she can feel it in the air, dissonant vibrations from the reversal of his blood flow.

But it can also happen from out of nowhere, even though she's right there the whole time. Sometimes she knows why – if something gets broken or if she forgets herself and says something about Mum. She's learned the signs, even the smallest ones. A twitch of the face. A shift in the voice. Sometimes it can be corrected, if you're quick about it. But each outburst always poorly conceals a promise of even greater rage.

She pictures a butterfly-like man with a black cape and antennae who slowly descends from the ceiling towards Dad's body while he's reading the newspaper. When he feels the antennae against his neck and turns he gets an eyeful of dark, evil stardust and this is what transforms him into his subterranean alter ego. Into a new source of gravity which methodically draws all the oxygen from the house. She tries to walk silently on tiptoe. The silver necklace hangs around her neck like a noose. Her skin turns numb from the cold metal.

She thinks about her promise.

That night, after the Friday evening film, she doesn't manage to escape in time. With his half-empty glass in his hand he turns towards her with damp lips. His heavy breathing is mechanical and the air around him pulses as he fixes her with his stare. A trembling mouse facing the snake.

'Why do you even come here?' he begins to intone.

He regards her with a darkened gaze from deep below the surface of his eyes.

This is before he begins to weep, that will come later. That's the worst. First, he was furious but hid it, let it grow in silence, dough soundlessly rising over the brim. She had been preoccupied with the film, sensing the growing tension in him but not realizing that it would progress so quickly. He must've started drinking earlier in the day. She hadn't been sufficiently observant.

His voice closes like a hand around her neck, intense, evil, oppressive. 'Why do you come here when you don't care about me anyway? You just want presents, you don't love me. I just give and give and you take. You're not my princess any more. You're just as cold as she is.'

She cannot speak. Sits on the very edge of the armchair with every muscle tensed to its limit.

The whites of the animals' eyes glisten with anxiety and they pull and wrench at her but she cannot move. She is held captive by his gaze. Dad's eyes are smooth and his cheeks oily, his mouth wet with saliva.

Kore's lungs compress within her; she is only exhaling at this point, nothing returns.

'Are you too special,' he slurs, clumsily placing his glass on the table, 'to talk with your dad?'

Suddenly his gaze seems to lose its balance, flitting towards the darkened window as a car passes the street. She is free. The animals help her to her feet and drag her away towards the basement stairs.

'Go then!' he says, and begins to snivel. 'Go ahead, just leave me here, alone… you little shit…'

She doesn't run, just walks briskly down the stairs. She remembers that her toothbrush is still up there. Skipping it once won't make a difference, her mum would say. But Kore doesn't want to think about her now; she turns the key and takes a seat on the bed to console her animals. Slowly strokes their fur until they stop trembling. The Long-fingered One climbs up her arm and falls asleep on her shoulder. The others yawn and arrange themselves in a pile on the blanket next to her, even Ivrahim. But Kore can't sleep.

If she had a sister they would sit with their arms around each other and weep. But it doesn't help to cry alone. The little dried pea has risen up into her throat, choking her like a clump that she can't get rid of despite swallowing and swallowing until her mouth turns dry. With her eyes on the door handle she grips the key in her fist. But he has one too. *In case there's a fire.* She listens for footsteps on the stairs but he doesn't follow her. After maybe twenty minutes she hears the front door close. A rubbish bin tips over as he backs the car out. Then all is quiet.

By around half past eleven the next day she is the most horrible child in all of Norrbotten. It's true. She sits at the kitchen table with her messy hands. Her father is in the chair opposite her in his robe, just out of bed, his large body heavier than usual. A viscous, acrid odour hangs in the air around him. Kore looks down at the table. Two halves of a pomegranate lie in front of her. They are everywhere in the house, set out in bowls, like a kind of bait. The heavy, meaty food filling the fridge can be difficult to eat, so this morning she took a piece of fruit. Sliced it in half with a large knife that lay in the second drawer. At first it didn't taste all that good but she got used to it. The juice looks like blood on her hands and on the teaspoon she uses to hollow out the fruit. The seeds are ruby red, like gemstones. They crunch as she chews them. In the centre of her tongue there is now a compacted mass of seeds that has grown until it fills her whole mouth. She wants to go and spit it out in the sink, but she doesn't because just then he enters the kitchen. Beside her on the table lies an old Bamse Bear comic that she had brought up from the basement. That's always the hardest thing, to walk back upstairs again. You don't know what's waiting for you. She doesn't dare leaf through the comic with her messy hands. Anyway, it's best to sit still now. She is the worst child in Norrbotten, abandoning her own father. Why doesn't she say anything when he speaks to her? Eventually she swallows the sharp ball of seeds.

For the rest of the day she and the animals keep to themselves in the basement. They are afraid and don't dare follow her up, telling her there are other animals in the house whom he let in during the night. Animals that are bigger than they are, and older, and more dangerous. Her father mows the lawn outside; she listens to the distant sound of the lawnmower through the narrow basement window high up near the ceiling. The summer light flickers through the boards. Only a week ago she was home with her mother.

Kore sits with the animals in her lap and one on her shoulder, in the large corner sofa covered in shiny black grained leather. His videos are arranged in a row on the shelf opposite her. She has watched almost all of them. Since Dad doesn't like cartoons he usually translates the dialogue for her so that she can watch his films instead, but it's difficult to understand anything besides the sharp sound of echoing gunshots, the dark blood slowly covering the floor, the long fingernail digging in a wound until it gets hold of the silver bullet and the man's screams as his steaming heart is plucked right out of his chest.

Mum phones every Tuesday and Friday. At the sound of the long rattling rings Kore leaps to her feet and starts running. But when she lifts the receiver and listens the voice is far away, scratchy. The little clump in her stomach has begun aching even more and Kore has difficulty concentrating. She doesn't answer her mother's questions properly, doesn't ask any herself. Her ankles feel exposed and cold up here. Only Titus and Masha followed her up, stopping on the last step of the basement stairs. Now they are crouched there, waiting for her to return. Her father is nowhere to be seen, the house holds its breath. Maybe he's standing with his back pressed against an adjoining wall, listening.

'I miss you so much, my little one,' Katja says.

Kore observes the slow dance of dust particles in a beam of light from the kitchen window without replying. Soon they hang up.

That night there's a party amid the dark greenery of the back garden, with metallic torches impaling everything that struggles to live, thrust into tree trunks and down into the soil. Taxi after taxi arrives and unloads, as nobody is planning to drive. Everyone is going to drink and toast along with her father, raising their glasses skyward together. A long, fully laid table extends towards a large fire into which he thrusts small flayed carcasses, sparks engulfing them like the burning eyes of the night. Guests laugh and feast with their greasy fingers and lips, calling out between bites for more. Her father talks and gurgles and drinks, standing near the fire as though he were in it. One of his eyes a strangler, the other an instigator. He watches his guests until they begin to move like waves. Every time the fire flares towards Kore they grasp at her with their fingers, the scent of meat wafting towards her throat, but she backs away, right through a gap in the hawthorn hedge. On the other side the air is cool. There's a little nook, a pergola.

She climbs up into the neighbour's old hammock and lies down, rocking carefully so that it doesn't squeak. She waves away the first mosquito that lands, but not the second.

Outside, the sky is blue and the sun shines bright white. Her father tells her to lie down on the sofa in the living room. A strange man stands next to him, someone he knows, a colleague named Kenneth. Dad pulls up her sweater and then opens her trousers so that the man can examine her. His hands sink into her stomach in two places at once. She has fallen ill again and eventually she had to tell him. But her affliction has a way of evading others' eyes. In her father's presence it's just like everything else with her, elusive. She shakes her head when the man asks if it hurts here, or here, or there. Kenneth moves his hand each time she says no. Dad's mouth is tense.

'I've taken her everywhere over the years – ultrasound, endoscopy.'

The colleague doesn't notice the clump, doesn't feel a thing. It's too small to be detected. Impenetrable now, smooth and dark. They pull her trousers a bit further down in order to feel the very lowest part of her stomach, exposing a few strands of pubic hair. Their eyes are immediately drawn to it. A damp snake slithers its way through Kore's insides; her palms begin to sweat. As rigid as a board, she clenches her jaw, bracing herself against wave after wave of shame that breaks over and engulfs her. But her father and the other one seem relieved. The pressure on her belly stops. 'Something premenstrual, presumably. Puberty. You might assume she's too young, but there you have it.' They carelessly tug her sweater back down and shake hands. Kore pulls up her trousers and slinks away.

As soon as she's out of the room she doubles over.

She has stowed all the presents on the shelf in her room. There's no room for the doll. She holds it indecisively against her chest while she has a look around. Its blonde hair is long, like a grown-up's. Its eyes roll back into its head when she looks at it. She holds it with her arm like a baby and tries to grab the eyelids, tries to close them. A tall shadow looms in the doorway. He stands there, half visible. The sun is low, its blinding light shining between the boards in the window, nearly gone. A glass hangs from his fingers, refracting the light like amber.

'Has your milk come in?' he says with a smirk.

Her face slowly melts off her head and runs down into the abyss, falling endlessly.

As soon as he is gone she hides the doll in the hallway cupboard beneath a few blankets. Back in her room she searches for her animals. Gets down on her knees and looks under the bed, lifting the duvet. She glances around the room, runs out into the hallway, into the room with the films, to the bathroom and back to her own room. She can't find them. Only the blank stares from the plastic animals on the shelf, with their smarmy painted-on smiles and synthetic fur. Her hands fumble across her own face. Under the smooth layer of rubber it's lumpy, like a crust of dried coal particles covering her skull.

She rubs and rubs.

*

That night everything accelerates quickly and endlessly slowly at the same time. It was already too late. She knew it. The bloodfruit, their verbal contract and her father's crying, swollen face.

'It's not like I raped you,' he says after a long silence.

She doesn't know why he says it, where it comes from. So that thought is in him after all? That look? She feels it at once, can't feel anything else. And he said it as though it was a defence. As though *if* he'd actually done it she would have the truth on her side. She could be examined, there would be marks. But no one will find the black clump, it's invisible to everyone.

She flees like a rabbit, the way she has always done. Down into the hole, deep underground.

She's awakened that night by the feeling of standing still in the middle of her darkened room, trying to grasp something. A sound she's heard. A distant, cold sound, like metal against porcelain. Against teeth. She's heard it before but she doesn't know where it comes from. The room is full of tentative shadows that shrink and swell. She walks slowly to the door, follows the walls along the hallway. The open bathroom door is a gaping rectangular hole of darkness; she continues past it, onward like a sleepwalker, mechanically, with her vision clouded as though she was underwater. Or underground. It's the weight of the earth she feels, the way it presses against the walls and ceiling. Faint sticky noises are the only sound as she lifts her sweat-dampened feet from the floor with each step. She knows exactly where to walk so that the floorboards won't creak. As though she's been up a thousand times in the night, heard a sound and walked out to investigate. Directly in front of her is the door to his office, so close and yet so far. It pulsates back and forth. A thin line of light escapes the slightly open door, which is usually locked. She catches a glimpse of him in there, big and heavy, bent over something. And she's behind him. When she sees his back the air becomes harder to breathe, a heavy wet sheet closes around her ribs, the air is suddenly cold when she inhales, as though she's swallowed a cough drop. She tries not to take in the air too quickly; the slightest sound will make him turn around and glare at her with glowing eyes, a chemical green in the thick darkness. His broad back is only a few metres away from her now, in his white doctor's coat, swaying back and forth as if he's laughing, his elbows occasionally flaring out to the side. He is bent over something, she can't see what. He has white rubber gloves on, beside him is a white tray of metal instruments. There are various pliers, forceps, scalpels – he moves more quickly, drops a tool and picks up another – the ones he leaves behind are bloody and now Kore's feet move towards him on their own, slowly, as though against the current.

And then she sees what's lying in front of him on the table. She sees it. She sees.

She presses her hands to her mouth to stop herself from screaming but her knees give way, wobbling as she sees those imploring eyes staring intently at her from the table, the one that never refuses, never speaks up, never says no, just yes, yes, yes, do what you want with me! She sees the childlike eyes, that pleading, scrawny little thing. And she backs out of the room, step by step, shhh, quietly, quietly, holds her mouth, her eyes locked to that stare, that stare, that most terrible of all stares. Back out in the hallway she turns round and runs, no longer caring about being heard, just needing to get away from there, back to her room, in time, but of course that's run out long ago.

Nobody knows where bravery comes from.

But eventually it comes.

Early in the morning she quietly calls the animals to her, trying one last time. Now they emerge, those that remain. Only two have survived. Titus's expression is blank as she strokes his back with her index finger. He seems unharmed. Ivrahim has been blinded in both eyes, as though someone has burned him with a glowing poker. Kore carefully lowers them into her rucksack and creeps out. She walks past all the houses; only one neighbour is awake. On the way back from his letter box he raises a hesitant hand in greeting. At the bus stop she mechanically takes out her money. Seven kronor buys her a ticket. After getting off at the station in her mother's town she walks directly to the phone booth, drops in another three shiny kronor and dials.

'Are you sure?' her mother asks when they're sitting in the car.

But Kore says nothing. Sure, how do you get to be that?

Afterwards everything is silent, not a word from her father's realm. He does not insist that she return, doesn't send anyone to fetch her. But every night she waits. Waits to see someone outside her window, a long finger reaching for her, digging and probing in her flesh, digging until it plucks out her steaming heart and breaks it open like a piece of fruit.

In her memory of him all his strength has been drained. If she closes her eyes she can see him, how he sits in his house at night. With the lamp turned off, the only light reaching him tumbles through the windows from the street lights outside.

His eyes are dry. *Crying to yourself doesn't help.* The cylindrical glass. Always careful with his coasters so that no rings are left on the Swiss side table. She remembers when he bought it, how proud he was. Everything he bought after that needed to match it. A rounded love seat the colour of dark-green avocado skin, the paintings in beige, dark brown, a similar green and occasional wine-red flecks. On the walls were the inherited silver candleholders. He never used them, worried he'd get wax spots on the smooth wooden floor.

She sees him sitting there completely alone. Sitting there staring at nothing. The light from the street in his eye, his mottled, cloudy eye.

For a long time afterwards she tries to pretend that he doesn't exist. Tries to forget the basement, his back turned to her, the creeping car. Imagines that none of it ever existed but, rather, belongs to one of a thousand evil stories that pour out of every book she touches. Because every book she reads, every film she sees, is about him. He retains that power. And every so often she thinks she sees him drive by in his silver car. Each time she turns completely cold, like being immersed in dark water, at the very moment that it penetrates her clothes.

Sometimes she thinks he is spying on her. That his tearful rage has become an obsession. That he's become psychotic, delirious, wild-eyed, is driving around in his car, searching, through days and nights, even beyond the border into brighter lands. That he has begun acting strangely among others too, started showing them his true nature. Been excluded from board meetings and eventually lost his position at the clinic. And now the neighbours see a strange green glow from his basement window at night. Toxic fumes escaping from every crevice. The basement itself remade into a laboratory.

And there he sits.

Night after night, intoning. Incantations to compel her to him. To ensnare her. His eyes have become dark holes. A sickly light emerges from the blackness. And then the little black clump in her begins to ache, awakens from its slumber and responds. *Yes, Daddy! I'm on my way!* Steam rises up from the clump right through her body, passing unhindered through her flesh as if through a perforated screen. It rises up to her eyes and all she can see is haze. The shadowland emerges from it, with its marshes and predators and the crowns of the trees like a black ceiling overhead. She has promised, after all. The clump remains, and the father within it, a concentrated, shrunken version of him whose defining parts are magnified, deeply imprinted and eternal.

In those moments when everything else recedes, his face looms before her. It is the only thing she sees. As though he has been sitting behind her the whole time, in the darkness. Waiting for her to stop running, turn round and finally understand that he will never leave. That she is and always will be his little queen. He is not the kind of person you leave, but, rather, one you walk towards. And he will rise up and take her, fill her up with the past.

With childhood once again.

And thus it was that she has created for herself a realm of her own, more desolate than his. In that place she is alone. And her realm is new but simultaneously ancient, for someone lived here long ago. Their tracks lie hidden in the moss. They have sunk ever further down, become one of the treasures among the layers of sediment.

This realm is the first and only landscape that she has got to know. Her father's face. She remains there, vigilant for the slightest twitch or tension, so that she can seek shelter in time.

She sees her footprints in the riverbeds along his cheeks where round teardrops used to drown out all life. Now the ground is desiccated, the tracks in the dry mud are cracked. She searches her way in among the eyebrows, which offer no protection against the sun. Her feet sink into the cheeks as though into quicksand. The safest place is at the summit of the cheekbone, in the fringes of forest at his temple. Thus it was before and thus it is now. On certain days she considers simply falling, when the silence echoes too loudly within her. But the height is breathtaking. So instead she chooses the opposite, a journey inward, into the black eye socket.

Should I call out? she wonders suddenly, but decides that it's safer to find her way in first, down into the hollow that leads deep behind the mask where she has been living until now. So she jumps. Once inside, her footsteps echo in the inner ear like water drops in a cave. She walks further in but slips, sliding down, down, until all light has vanished.

She begins to hear a terrible sound, dull and rhythmic. It intensifies as she reaches the edge of the voice box. The wind heaves against her, softer from behind, stronger on its way back up. She crouches and tries to climb down the tracheal rings, but with only half her body dangling over the precipice everything is suddenly shaken into chaos by a cough and she loses her grip and falls headlong.

She falls and falls.

Life is suddenly only this falling.

She lands with a dull thud on an elastic membrane. In the centre is a tightly bound opening. Acid sloshes in the abdomen below her. Down here the sound is stronger and she knows which way to go. She backs up towards the wall and begins pressing her arms against its softness. First resistance, then the wall gives way. Maybe he knows. Maybe he can feel her now. She crawls for a long time through tissue, the sound more muffled, the flesh shuddering. Then she feels her fingers pass through, out into something else. A void. She grips the edges and pulls her body through.

The deafening beats are hurled at her.

And there it is. The machine. Blackened red, convulsive. Dad's heart. She had always imagined it as so much smaller, barely visible to the naked eye. But she was wrong. It's gigantic.

She tries to force in a leg but the muscle's violent contractions knock her away. Then she takes a running start and jumps straight at it with outstretched arms and legs, sticks to it with a sucking sound, presses her face right through the muscular wall, and as if by magic her whole body slides through.

Inside everything is silent.

No wind comes, because there is no wind. Is that it? Is there only this darkness here?

But then something floats into view. It's a body, a small one, sleeping. Swaddled in cloth, it floats closer and closer.

It's a child.

Is it me? she thinks. Is it me floating through your heart?

She wants to see herself in the child's face. But the features are so nondescript that she forgets them as soon as she blinks. Like the picture in a new frame before you exchange it for your own.

She tries, after all of this, to write a letter, but she sounds and expresses herself like a little child, without knowing what she wants to say. Or what he should reply. After all, she's the one who left. She glues a dried flower to the letter, a pale-blue forget-me-not, but she doesn't post it. The letter sounds too helpless, pleading. Something else is needed.

As the years pass she begins to dream about growing tall and fearsome. Cold, cautious, powerful. And she dreams of the day when he finally comes crawling. She wouldn't even react when he entered, instead she'd finish writing her very long sentence, calmly set down her pen and regard him, her face expressionless.

'Yes?'

No more than that, after his long journey to catch a glimpse of his long-lost child. *Yes?* And he will tremble in her presence, feel anxious and simultaneously be filled with wonder at her transformation. From a little ten-year-old with eyelashes full of tears to this *creature* – so preoccupied and dangerous. She'll watch him with calm eyes as he presents his case for reconciliation, and she'll let him conclude without interrupting, then tell him in honeyed tones, 'There is no mercy for people like you.'

She had thought this through carefully, this 'people like you', because it showed that she knew that he was a certain *type* – the type who always cared more about himself than about his own child. That one sentence would make him understand, and regret. And then the dust would disperse, the thorns around his house would disintegrate and be scattered to the wind, and everything would be different.

That is how it must end.

But time passes. And he doesn't come.

Nothing is as it should be.

Finally she goes to him, secretly, in disguise. This time she travels alone, in a borrowed car that can accelerate rapidly. He has a new job in a clinic in one of the grey high-rises in the city centre. But the town looks different now, like any other town, with a shopping area and a car park and a pond with a fountain in the middle. No one pays any attention to her, or even recognizes her. She pulls off her hood and has a look around in the pale afternoon light.

The journey teaches her two things: he has both a new car and a new family. A new wife and a little daughter. In fact, she has hardly looked at him, because as soon as she sees him lift the new child from the back of the car and walk hand in hand with her into the toy shop, she doesn't have eyes for anyone else. The girl – small and blonde with curls and peekaboo eyes – looks nothing like Kore. She hides like a dirty old man, staring at the sweet child, as though waiting for the first opportunity to capture her in a black sack and carry her out into the woods. Cut off her hair. Drown her in some pond. And later when the search party comes across the dead little girl she'll be all pale and muddy, her curls straightened out into ugly strands.

But that too would turn out wrong, because Dad would weep and raise his hands to the sky. And he would hold the dead child in his arms and rock her back and forth as though she were only sleeping, but her dark-blue eyes would stare blindly.

Kore would see all of it, crouched behind a stump or an uprooted tree, and know that it hadn't made anything better, because now he would grieve that beloved child for all eternity, the child that never betrayed him. And later Kore would look down at her own hands and see they had become grey, scaly and slimy, soil-stained, with rough claws instead of nails.

She opens her mouth to yell but no sound emerges. Her throat makes a clicking sound, reptilian, nothing more. When the new wife has left to do some shopping and Kore's father drives away, she follows the car, through the city and out to his domain. The river is steel grey, lifeless, empty. Then she's back at his house, just as simple as that. He is standing in the driveway, waiting, as if he knew all along.

'Come and say hello now,' he says straight away, as she warily steps out of the car.

He waves gently and she follows him, as she always has. Then he takes her inside with him. Her little sister is sitting there playing with Kore's old toys. The black plastic horse, the doll, the wheel, all the bracelets, the boxes. Glass marbles, the puzzle and the other animals.

'She's finally come,' Dad shouts, so loudly that the girl is startled.

Kore asks him to stop, says that he's frightening her, but he just laughs at that. Then they watch as the child arranges her plastic animals in a ring around her, at perfect angles to her. The animals regard the girl with frightened plastic eyes until she gets angry and kicks them all over. Dad ushers Kore into the living room and offers her juice. She'd rather have coffee but he doesn't care about that.

Some things never change.

And as she takes a seat on the very edge of the armchair, with a furtive glance at the nursery, her fingers tightly wrapped around the glass so that he can see that she still bites her nails, just like she used to, he opens his mouth to speak.

And he says, 'When I was born my dad planted a tree that was supposed to grow at the same pace as I did, and later when I died that tree was to be chopped down so that the growth rings could be counted, and then I would be able to see how many of my years I'd lived happily. Because that's the only time trees grow, my dad told me.'

'Is the tree still around?' Kore asks.

But then his face vanishes into a dark hole that sucks everything into itself, a vacuum mouth that rips at her clothes, tears at her skin. He and this hole-face begin to grow, turning a grey-blue colour and swelling up towards the ceiling until his neck is bent into one of the corners of the room. He squeezes her out of the room; she has to run to get away, to avoid being sucked back into the hole. Something moves up and out of her gullet, something burning hot, a little black clump that is sucked out of her body and vanishes, as she grabs hold of the door frame at the very last moment and manages to pull herself out of the room. Kore throws open the front door and is outside.

On her way to the car she catches sight of the tree, just as he described it, in the shadow of the house. A wretched little thing that she'd never noticed before, with a sickly pale trunk and strange dark-red blossoms. And from the tree she hears a low whistling sound that follows her into the car and settles on the rubber mat at her feet, like an animal that has been lost for a long time but has at last found its way home.

The Girlfriend

The worry was always at its worst in the afternoons, when it squeezed its sweaty fingers around Anna's body and little threads of unease slithered relentlessly within her muscles.

Sometimes it happened as early as twenty past three. It began to appear as a shadow in the corner of her eye. If she stood in front of the mirror she could almost see how it had found its way into her, made her contours hazy, as if someone had erased a thick pencil mark just there but hadn't got all of it. David never got home before half past six, she knew that. Nevertheless, something got her to her feet. Got her to start pacing, like an animal preparing to give birth. Her heart pounded within her, her cheeks alternately flushed and lost their colour repeatedly. She wrapped her arms around her body and stood still. Watched the scene unfold with her mind's eye: him opening the front door, the eyes, the brown hair and the attractive hands. And she knew that he was a completely ordinary human being after all. All of it was so odd, the way it had come to be.

Anna typically endured, forced herself to stay at the computer until five o'clock, although she never got anything more done. It wasn't as though the worry came as early as twenty past three every day. Not often at all, normally, although occasionally several times a week. She got behind in her assignments.

She couldn't talk about it with her friends, they wouldn't understand. She couldn't even say that they wouldn't understand because then they'd think she was full of herself. As if she, after just a few months with some guy, might experience something that they *couldn't even understand*. They, who'd had so many 'adventures' and met so many 'engrossing' people. She didn't want to be one of *those* whom she used to laugh at a little. One of those like both of her friends, who could chatter on for so long about the latest in an endless stream of infatuations that they grew unbearable. Each one of them was the most *fantastic* person they'd ever met – eventually the word was so played out that it sounded almost profane. There were no words left. So she kept to herself.

They wouldn't understand.

For how could she explain that sometimes, when she looked at David, it felt like she was going to die? It was completely different from any other feeling she'd ever had. She had only heard people describe love in these terms when talking about their children: 'When my daughter was born everything changed.'

When she met David everything had changed.

It was difficult to put a finger on exactly how. And she couldn't say anything to him about it either; instead she held back as much as she could because she knew that if she opened the door more than just a crack, everything in there, all the words and feelings, would burst out and drown him. And he would gasp for oxygen and then everything would be over.

But at the same time as she'd needed to start struggling seriously to avoid letting everything out at once, to focus instead on letting it trickle out a little at a time, this worry had sought solace in her body. And it had woven itself well into her. Now it was everywhere.

Sometimes she had difficulty sleeping. She would lie awake and watch him as he slept, listen to his breathing and eventually become almost desperate and start thinking hateful things, like: 'What is it that's so special about you that makes me act like this?' And it was difficult to determine what it was that caused this all-consuming condition she found herself in. Sure, she admired him, thought he was beautiful and funny and so on, but he wasn't the most beautiful person she knew, just the one she loved the most.

Occasionally she thought it was just an illusion, a high. That she'd soon wake up and feel only emptiness when she looked at him. That she'd overloaded their relationship – overloaded him – because she'd wished so intensely to meet someone who would, you know, shake up her whole being.

Yet David was always so calm and considerate. It was one of the first details she'd noticed about him, the way he moved his hands through the air – gently, with a kind of elegance. Even from his hands you could see that he was intellectual. And at night, when those hands rested softly on the blanket, she sometimes couldn't resist edging closer to smell them. Sometimes she let her tongue come out of her mouth, just a little, so that she could lick one of his knuckles. Close her lips around it, tenderly, like a nursing baby. Then she could sleep.

But OK, then there was that thing with the chair.

Because they were upgrading the plumbing in her apartment, she'd moved in with David. It had been too early to move in for real, they both thought so. But since it was only going to be for a short while it seemed OK. To tell the truth, Anna had almost changed her mind. Because it had got worse, the worry, since she'd moved in.

You see, she had placed a chair with its back against the wall in the living room, just around the corner as you look in from the hall. And when the worry came she'd taken to sitting there. But it was difficult to keep still, she needed to walk, so she was constantly getting up and needing to do something. Her hands might look dry or there was an email she'd forgotten to send. Maybe she saw a spot of dried tomato sauce on the stove next to the knob controlling the largest ring, and all it took was a few wipes with the dishcloth for it to be gone.

Why she'd placed the chair just there – as close as possible to the front door yet still out of sight – she couldn't say. Before, she used to linger by the kitchen window, and at least there you could see outside (even if their entrance was on the other side). She could look down into the red and green playground, watch the aspen leaves flutter towards the ground and decay into a soggy mat. But that was long ago.

Lately she had almost exclusively sat in the chair.

And in it, time stood still. At least the clock on the stove did, suggesting that it was 15:45, though she was sure it had said the same thing the first time she'd looked. But that would be totally crazy.

She felt like drinking a glass of wine but it was still light outside and she couldn't bring herself to do it. Plus she had so much to do, couldn't she just sit down and get on with it without all this carry-on? She made an attempt. Walked over and opened the document on the computer, held her hands out in front of herself, as if to hinder something from rushing towards her – but it was impossible. Her hands refused to touch the keyboard. She could feel it physically within her body, permanently lodged in there.

The worry.

Its slightest movement set her off; at even the slightest vibrations she could almost hear a squeaking sound, like rubber against a wet glass, while it wound itself deeper into her cramped insides. As if she were the one writhing her way through herself, seeking air, pressed between two organs that resembled the thick red mats in the school gymnasium. The liver, the intestines. The heart.

In truth, David most often came home before half past six, despite the fact that he probably wanted to stay longer. Unlike her he wasn't a morning person and preferred to work late into the night. She actually thought it was romantic – she could picture him alone at the university, the warm light of his desk lamp illuminating his beautiful hands.

But since Anna had moved in he tried to get home as early as possible so that they could cook together, which they both enjoyed. She had to try hard to avoid having everything ready when he came home, partly for that reason, but also so that he wouldn't think she was any less busy or consumed by her tasks than he was by his work. This was normally true, but not any more. Now she found herself in this upside-down world in which she was ashamed of her behaviour and somehow proud at the same time, for enduring so diligently, living silently through the transformation that had befallen her these last few months. And in certain moments when it all felt right on the edge of being too much trouble, she encouraged herself to keep struggling. Calm would come with time. Isn't that how it usually goes? The rush of infatuation, then a calmer, more secure love.

As if she had a choice.

But this strange new world also granted entry to voices that described the situation differently, implying that it was embarrassing the way she carried on. That she was acting 'like a child' by sitting and waiting in that way, and 'if he only knew…' But worst of all was that other word, the one that hid its ugly snout inside her, that eventually got hold of the edges of the door frame and hauled itself in. Its fat body slipped through, landing with a wet thud. And now the word was there, out in the open.

Pathetic. That she was pathetic.

The very fact that she sat *out of view* of the door, that was the worst. So that she could silently stand up, grab the chair with one hand, scurry out to the kitchen to replace it and then go to say hi. All that took approximately the same amount of time as it would have done if she'd actually sat at the computer in the kitchen, finished writing her sentence, saved the document, stood up and then simply walked into the hallway (perhaps still consumed by thoughts from her work and therefore moving somewhat hesitatingly) and said, 'Hi, David,' or just, 'Hi.' He smiled, happy to see her, and even if she actually wanted to run over and hug him – her whole insides felt like a closed fist of pent-up love – she always managed to preserve her cool-but-in-love smile and remain calm, to allow something more appropriate to seep out, and that'd be enough.

But on the days when it plagued her the most, when the worry came before four o'clock and it was almost three hours until he'd be home, and she was stuck in this utterly lonely and helpless state, it was very difficult to have a relaxed conversation when he finally arrived.

Sometimes it felt like she was going to start crying.

She wished out loud that just once, just one time, she could see him shaken and upset. Hear him off balance because of her. For if that happened, everything would feel lighter, she was sure of it. Then she'd know with confidence that *he too*…

When the worry emerged it brought out the very worst in her, thoughts like 'it's completely different for him' and that she was 'abnormal' for feeling this strongly.

That she was going crazy.

'You can't even concentrate on your work,' the voice whispered to her. 'You can't function normally any more and you're keeping everything secret, even from your friends. Don't you know that it's unhealthy to hide things like this – as though you were an alcoholic or a *junkie*, hiding your feelings like bottles of booze?'

Once those thoughts had established themselves it wasn't worth even trying to get anything done any more. Nothing to be done but go straight to the chair and let them circulate within her however they wanted to, while she alternately agreed and resisted, all in the name of variety, to make the time go faster, so that he would come home and make everything all right again.

She couldn't relax in the chair, wouldn't slouch even momentarily, despite her perfect positioning – she could hear the slightest sound from the stairwell, she was out of sight, could see the clock on the stove, its digital numbers glowing green, and besides there was plenty to look at in the living room. David was interested in art. She was never bored, occupying herself instead with finding new details in the images.

She liked all of the paintings, except for one that portrayed a dog. It was one of those breeds that is obedient and eager to please, a cocker spaniel maybe. The painting was composed as a portrait, the dog glancing pitifully at the observer. There was a sense of shame about its whole posture, half turned as if it knew that it was supposed to move out of the way, relinquish its spot to a real human. Something in its eyes shone out of the painting and tightened the grip of worry around Anna's throat. As a result she tried not to look in that direction. For there was something meek and submissive shining in the dog's eyes.

The Slave Gaze, Anna called it. Helpless at its master's feet.

Please like me! it implored every time she happened to look towards it, and it nauseated her.

So she'd tried to get David to take down that particular painting. Without saying it directly, of course, it was his home after all and she didn't want to become one of those people who showed up and started throwing their weight around. She'd rather die. But David liked the painting, even called the dog Li'l Frans and occasionally tried to cheer him up with a little joke. In moments like that it was hard for Anna to keep quiet, to avoid screaming and throwing something right at the idiotic picture, destroying it. Luckily she never did that. She just smiled weakly at his joke. Then she changed the subject.

Time passed, on this day as on all the others. She had her usual routes. The chair, the computer, the chair, the window, the chair, the bathroom, the chair, the computer, the chair, the fridge, the chair, the computer, the chair. At a quarter to seven she started to worry.

Maybe something had happened. A car accident; head-on collision on the motorway?

Accidents were always happening there and she thought about how difficult it could be for the emergency services to arrive in time. People grew impatient in traffic and tried to pass, which kept the ambulances from reaching the injured.

She tried to calm herself. Fifteen minutes is nothing, she thought. Maybe he was held up by some casual acquaintance in a conversation he couldn't escape as quickly as he'd like to. There were loads of plausible reasons for a fifteen-minute delay. That calmed her down a bit.

Suddenly she realized that she was sitting in darkness. The sun must've set hours ago. After she'd turned on the lights in the living room she went into the bathroom and looked at herself in the mirror, added a little blusher and returned to the chair. Checked her mobile. Five minutes to seven.

She felt a hint of cramp at the base of her spine from sitting there so tensely and tried to force her body into a more relaxed position.

But it was difficult. Her insides felt like a cluster of knots and they tightened with every breath, increasing her body's density as though she were a spring that might uncoil at any moment. Because soon her mobile would ring, an unknown number, and a serious voice would ask if she was related to David Holmström, and then everything would be over. She would die right there and then and people would say that they hadn't believed it until now, but that she was the proof, that you could die of a broken heart.

She looked at her mobile again. Two minutes past.

A sound caused the knots to tighten further. The lift door opened. Steps on the tiled floor. Her teeth began to ache. But weren't those steps a little too shuffling? David walked so fluidly, somehow, not sloppily like that.

She was right. A cough revealed that it was a neighbour. That lazy character in the woolly hat. The footsteps faded further down the corridor.

Anna swallowed, though her mouth was totally dry. In her mind's eye she could see the flashing blue lights reflected in a pool of blood on the motorway's autumn-dampened tarmac. But maybe he wasn't quite dead yet. Maybe he would manage a word, just one more, to the first person who reached him and saw the crack in his bright white skull. The dark blood slowly forming a halo around his head. And the brain matter scattered like stars around him. Another driver who leaped from his car and rushed over to the mangled body saw him lying there and thought, 'How can he still be alive? Is he watched over by angels?' But the explanation came soon enough, for the message David forced out with his last breath, sacrificing all his strength to utter it, revealed all.

Anna!

And in that word, as he lay there and died, in that word was everything. It would be the replacement for all the words she had missed, it would be eternally sufficient. And she would know that *he too…*

But then she snapped back to reality again. Someone else was coming. The wheezing sound of the lift doors sliding open. Footsteps again, the familiar echo. Could it be…? Didn't that sound just like his boots, precisely his pace, his weight? An escalating tremor flooded her body. Now she heard the sound of keys, *his* keys.

There was no longer any doubt.

It bubbled up in her, happiness pounded through her body, rushed up her neck and out into her arms, down her legs. He isn't dead. *Not dead! Not dead!* He's home! He is fi-na-lly home! She stood up quickly and laid her hand on the chair, ready to carry it into the kitchen, but decided to forget it. Just this once.

Her body was a million explosions, effervescent, her heart throbbed, her eyes popped in their sockets. Today the chair didn't really matter. She could always say that she had used it to try to chase out a fly, or whatever, she didn't care because now he opened the door and came in.

It was very difficult not to rush straight out there. Despite the fact that she couldn't see him she knew precisely in what order he did everything. First he took off his mittens and hat, then he made space on the clothes rail, took off his jacket and hung it on a hanger. After that he unwound his scarf and bent down to untie his shoelaces. She saw it clearly before her. Saw his melancholy posture, the beloved face, his calm movements, the furrowed brow (as though he was still pondering some academic problem he'd encountered during the day), the locks of hair at his temples, the hands.

The hands!

She struggled with all her might to avoid going out into the hallway, not yet. It was still too soon. If she'd been in the kitchen she could've shouted, 'Hi', *but not from here*. It was too close, she was forced to wait a little longer, as though she was finishing a sentence now and saving the document, getting up from the kitchen chair and starting to walk towards the hallway. She stood there watching herself, her invisible twin, as she walked past, then from the corner of her eye she saw that awful dog looking at her and it made her queasy, forcing her to swallow a violent surge in her throat, and that set her in motion, she started walking, following herself, slowly.

She rounded the corner.

David was standing there just as expected, bent over his shoes. When she saw him everything within her began gasping for oxygen, wanting to go to him, overwhelm him, all her words, all her emotions willed their way towards him so much that it ached.

But she held back, forcibly. Clenched her body like a knot of muscles, a bony imaginary hand squeezing her throat hard, closing it. She wanted to keep it ever so slightly open, thinking maybe it would be OK to let out a little bit more this time. It was dangerous, incredibly dangerous to say too much. She couldn't trust herself. But still, maybe today something just a little bigger than usual. Hadn't she earned that after having sat there half dead with fear? Maybe an 'I missed you'. Yes, she had. But nothing more!

The knots tightened, she felt half strangled and happy at the same time. He still hadn't seen her and she fought to walk slowly, placing one foot in front of the other, as if traversing a tightrope along the edge of a chasm, weighing her steps carefully though she really wanted to rush ahead. Fly into his arms.

Not dead! Not dead!

A sighing sound broke the silence, a little pop, and then she began to collapse inward. The knots were loosening, she noticed with surprise, and she wondered if she was about to faint. But she didn't, she was just rapidly approaching the floor.

Like a jacket falling off its hook.

She landed softly on all fours, noticing that the rug looked dusty and that it smelled a little mildewed. Then she raised her eyes and looked towards David, who had straightened back up. His shoes were untied but he hadn't yet stepped out of them. Instead he stood there and stared at her. She almost laughed because he looked so astonished.

But she didn't have time, the urgency overcame her.

Everything came at once. And for the first time she gave herself permission. She rushed right at him, and she felt so strong and beautiful with the sudden courage that came over her that she flew into his arms, or at least she tried to, she stretched herself up towards his face, wanted to overwhelm him with kisses – if only she could reach a little higher – just a little more!

But David backed away. Retreated towards the front door. His mouth opened soundlessly. Not a single word.

She sank back down onto her haunches and sat there.

But then, slowly, as if waking from a dream, he got down on one knee in front of her. He took her in his hands, lifted her slowly up into his arms and laid his cheek against her head. When he stroked her body and murmured something, against her neck, she began to lick his face. Licking, licking. And with each stroke of her tongue she felt better, so happy that her whole body trembled, finally able to show him. Finally able to be.

'Everything is all right now,' she thought. 'Everything is finally as it should be.'

On the Nature of Angels

He awoke to the opening and closing of his own mouth, over and over, as if he was a fish. His body felt cloudy inside, a vibrating silence just beneath his skin.

Something had happened.

His vision still blurry, he groped across the bedside table, knocking both his mobile phone and yesterday's crossword puzzle onto the thick rug before he got a hand on his notebook and managed to locate his last entry. Alas, nothing new. His head sank back onto the pillow. It was half past four in the morning, still dark outside. He had felt certain, without really knowing about what exactly. The memory of a voice, a figure. Someone who had called to him, standing just behind him and off to the side, surrounded by a blindingly dark glow. The thunderous power of water falling from high above. But the feeling wasn't a good one, wasn't benevolent.

Rising onto one elbow, he took hold of the notebook once again, browsing aimlessly at first, then letting the pages fall one at a time, slowly. That's when he saw it, written in a hasty scrawl across a page towards the middle of the book. Sleep-writing in black ink. He had to find his glasses to read it and when he did his heart began to pound. It was as though the power had switched on in his head. He had waited so long, but here it was. The message from the dream:

One day the night turns white

He didn't recognize the phrase. Maybe just a fragment left over at the end of a day's reading, an errant line from some poetry collection? But no.

This time it felt different.

The notebook was a diary of time spent waiting, rather like a bus stop. Training himself in lucid dreaming was a long-term strategy, with a clearly articulated aim. He was certain that they were invisible to humans, only revealed themselves on other planes, and that dreams were a potential way in. Nights had thus become at least as important to his scientific work as days.

The land of dreams.

He had been searching there since he was ten years old. One rainy summer's day, tired of his tattered back issues of *The Phantom*, he got hold of a random book from his parents' bookcase. *The Illustrated Children's Bible*. He devoured it in one go. There was another Jakob! And after having located his name, he even found his purpose: 'Then the angel of God said to me in the dream, "Jacob", and I said, "Here I am!"'

*

When Jakob arrived at his office it was just after nine in the morning. A restlessness teemed within him; his hands moved spider-like across the stacks of paper on his desk. He plucked the notebook from his breast pocket and thumbed through it. There it was again. *One day the night turns white.* The handwriting seemed unfamiliar. He rocked in his seat while waiting for the computer to start up.

There was a knock at the door and the department chair's head appeared.

'Can I come in?'

Harald's face had an odd hue to it, a deep purple that glowed through his skin. As though he had a habit of standing in his office, shouting at the top of his lungs, his neck tensed and face contorted, and then quickly collecting himself before walking out.

'Absolutely. Come in,' said Jakob, straightening in his chair.

A shaft of sunlight squeezed its way through the blinds and grazed the corner of his eye, making him blink.

'I'm sure you know' – Harald arranged himself in the guest chair – 'that things have been pretty tight the last few years.'

His relaxed face made him appear indifferent. Jakob made a confused attempt to wave the sunbeam out of his eye.

'Financially,' Harald continued, looking around the room.

Jakob pressed his lips together briefly and then leaned over his desktop to escape the glare.

'But there are plenty of students,' he replied. 'My classes are full this term, maybe even fuller than usual.'

'It's not about the students,' Harald interrupted. 'It's the distribution of teaching hours. There's going to be yet another consolidation next term and the cuts are unfortunately going to be comprehensive.'

'Ah,' said Jakob, withdrawing slightly.

The sunbeam immediately returned, piercing.

'There'll be more cutbacks among adjunct positions.'

Harald formed his words so far forward in his mouth that it took the shape of a beak. A fleshy little beak that opened and closed as he continued speaking.

Two summers ago, in early August, while trying to cross the street, Jakob had caught sight of Harald. He was standing on the bustling periphery of a colourful parade wearing a fishnet tank top and a pair of very short cut-off denim shorts. Jakob had stopped in his tracks, fascinated by the department chair's skinny, knobbly chicken legs, which stood in contrast to a rotund midsection bulging unshakeably over the waistband of his shorts. Harald was swaying slightly, back and forth, in time to a different tune from the one emanating from the parade, his eyes surveying the street and the cheering dancers on their glittering floats. At the office there was always a bureaucratic reserve about him, a melancholy. Oddly enough, Jakob felt caught off guard, seeing him happy.

'Jakob? Did you hear what I said?'

The octopus-beak mouth was still now. *Your contract expires in January*. His moustache was very dark and bushy. The students apparently referred to him as The Broom. Jakob looked down at his hands, which were resting in his lap like empty bird's nests.

'Of course.' Jakob shook his head slightly. His peripheral vision was still a little blurry.

'Good,' said Harald. He stood up and brushed a speck of invisible dust from his trousers.

Jakob rose halfway out of his chair, then sat down again. 'Not even hourly work...'

'I know,' said Harald. 'I understand that it'll be hard to get grants. Worst-case scenario, you'll have to change your focus for a while. You must have some other subject developing alongside your...'

His hand came to rest on the door handle, that straight smile sliced across his face.

'... alongside your special interest.'

Jakob said nothing.

'Good,' said Harald. 'We'll talk more later. I have to go and tell Lena now. Do you know if she's around?'

After he left, Jakob remained in his chair, his insides shrivelling like crumpled scraps of paper succumbing to a flame. But then he remembered last night and turned to the computer. He watched the quote of the day scroll past on his screen saver:

> *In Psalms, the poor man called and the Lord heard him and*
> *he saved him out of all his troubles, for the angel of the Lord*
> *encamps around those who fear him, and he delivers them.*

He let it scroll three times across the screen, then he lightly touched the mouse.

Seen from above he probably appeared rather small, shrunken, pathetic, in that moment before he drew a preparatory breath, before the double doors opened to let them in.

The horde.

They had been waiting a good long while out there, in crowded queues. Methodically pressing forward, sucking the oxygen from each other's mouths. A restless thumping on the doors and through the walls a muffled murmuring.

Inside everything was very quiet. The auditorium's empty space unfolded behind him. The semicircular rows of tip-up seats waited in perfect symmetry on either side of the aisle. Like two halves of a ribcage with empty lungs, the moment before an inhalation.

This is the worst time, he thought, placing each of his hands on its respective door handle. The first day of term.

He lightly squeezed the cold metal. But then he was startled by something and turned to the right. For an instant he thought he'd seen someone standing there, diagonally behind him, causing his windpipe to collapse slightly from a sudden vacuum. A dark shadow, a silhouette of something unfamiliar. It had noticed him hesitate.

The minute hand on his watch showed three minutes to ten. It was time.

He slowly drew his deep breath. Let it reach fully into his lungs and turn around, flow back out. Before the air had totally left him he pressed both of his hands down at the same time and opened the doors to the auditorium.

As the students poured in, so quickly that he had to take his first steps towards the whiteboard sideways, he contemplated how strange things had become. All the years of silence and thoughts had shrunk him; that secretive space around every person that defined them as human, it had sort of thinned out around him. People had begun walking right into his body. Like now, as they filled up every inch of the rows of seats. The noise in the room seemed to just grow louder.

Even after they took their seats they were linked together two by two, facing each other, engaged in lively conversation. Waved their antennae towards each other, chirped, shone in the afternoon light from the windows. Here and there someone hung over the row of chairs in front of them and formed a triangle, linked together by their hind parts like mating wasps. Although it was now a few minutes past ten, they continued talking. It was like this every year. And Jakob waited them out, with sweaty palms. Waited them out with the patience of an angel.

He propped himself against the table down by the whiteboard, with his arms crossed over his chest. His jacket was unbuttoned. The humans in front of him were a single, mobile individual. Kaleidoscopic, quivering.

A swarming anthill.

His eyes couldn't focus, found no single point to anchor to. For a moment he almost panicked. Blinking, he straightened up, let his arms drop towards the smooth wooden floor and regained some degree of control over his vision. His eyes cleared as he opened them as widely as possible, and in the moment that they came back fully under his control he noticed one of the students in the second row.

Uneven black pageboy haircut, jeans like everyone else, notebook like everyone else. Then he realized that it was because she was looking at him that she stood out. She sat completely still looking right at him, in the midst of the teeming mass. A thin silver thread stretched between their pupils, right through the room. She was the eye of the storm and her gaze was calm and steady, as if to say *It will be all right.*

A little smile flickered across her round face, which seemed almost boneless, in the way that people can look when they were chubby in childhood and have begun growing out of it a little too late. No structure yet, just a shape. Jakob made a croaking sound. The murmur settled slowly into a rustling sound as they opened their notebooks. The mass solidified. Her face merged into the crowd. He began.

'OK,' he said. 'Welcome to part one, an introduction to the history of religion: theory and methodology. If anyone has found their way to the wrong classroom, this is your chance to leave…'

Thirty minutes into the lecture, just as he placed an image on the overhead projector, he thought he heard a whisper:

'…who's called Dr Angelicus…!'

His head whipped around, his gaze scanning the rows of benches. Must've heard wrong. Everyone was new here. He continued. His pulse pounded in his throat but his words found their way into the proper order. The hands of the clock chopped methodically onward.

From time to time he saw her out there. Her round cheeks and little bichon frise chin, the soot-coloured hair. Within her that voice.

It will be all right.

The theologists kept to themselves at the far end of the left wing of the building. There weren't many of them. A few philosophers of religion and exegetes, a church historian and a young woman involved in interdisciplinary work who was usually in Copenhagen. Jakob's office was behind an anonymous light-grey door with a little nameplate that read 'Jakob Alm, Senior Lecturer', at the very end of the hall. Although he'd walked that hallway for many years, lately, whenever he saw a student, he felt an impulse to press his back against the wall, pass through it and disappear.

There goes the angelican, he imagined they thought. They saw his dark, dusty sports jacket, shoes that needed to be replaced. His clean, dry, wavy hair and his face, recognizable by the round metal frames of spectacles and nothing else. Easy to mistake for a wall.

The university treated the theologists like an appendage, an accessory to the History faculty. In Jakob's case the situation was even more precarious. In the 80s, when he'd completed his doctorate, he had published quite a bit. But the resistance was massive. He was the only one in the country conducting research into his vestigial branch of the field (there were a few in his subject area in the US, one or two Italians and a handful of others around the world, but no one he'd ever met, only those he'd read about, voraciously), which was angelology – the study of angels.

'This is simply not science,' people said, always continuing in the same contemptuous tone, 'more like *parapsychology*.' And then the conversation always found its way to the lack of *physical evidence*. Once, his opponent in a debate (a well-regarded historian of science) had even included a vulgar sketch of a supposed angel in their series of pro/con articles. 'In order to fly, angels would need to have such oversized shoulders that they would violate both the law of gravity and fundamental anatomical principles.'

All of Jakob's responses were abstractions and they rarely made an impact. He tried to explain that his research was more informed by literature, that angels existed in the interstitial spaces, in the gaps between the knowable. It's not about belief or the laws of physics but rather a condensed reality, concentrated moments when the layers of consciousness meet in a node and everything becomes clear. Angels move through those hidden spaces just like a piece of impenetrable poetry. Remaining invisible, incomprehensible, until someone learns to see them. It's about how one asks the questions, he tried to explain, not about gravity.

That's how it went. With time he lost heart.

After his slow retreat from academic debates he had all the peace and quiet he needed for his work. Everything calmed down. He supported himself by teaching, more classes than he could manage actually. Every new face, every new pair of eyes, settled on his shoulders. Over the years it had begun to weigh on him. And of course students had occasionally happened to find out about his area of expertise and asked him if it was true *that he believed in angels*? The first time he was asked that question, in the early 90s, he'd been so thrown that he hadn't managed to soften his tone when he replied with the counter-question: 'Do all theologists believe in God?' At some point he was given his hated nickname. No one said it aloud, but he heard it second-hand.

Dr Angelicus.

*

While he fished out his keys from his jacket pocket to unlock his office door the student adviser appeared. Lucy was thin, dark, pretty. A kind of coordinator for the whole institution. Her shoes were black and shiny, low-heeled. The design reminded him a little of the 70s, his mum's best shoes in the closet.

'I heard,' she said.

He raised his eyes and saw that she had tilted her head slightly to one side. Otherwise her face was as neutral as always. Harald once called her 'the cyborg'. She had integrity and that made a distinct impression. No one would ever presume to put an arm around her or give her a friendly thump on the back. Or even pat her on the shoulder.

Jakob liked her.

He nodded and attempted a smile, but his gaze met hers and bounced away. Every so often a soft-spoken man would pick her up towards the end of the day. They resembled each other somewhat, possibly he was her brother. On those days she left right away, once even forgetting to lock the door, so Jakob had seen that the papers on her normally immaculate desk had been left unsorted.

His throat tightened a little. Lucy coughed almost soundlessly and handed him a few pieces of paper.

'The last of the attendance lists,' she said.

'Thanks.'

He had to force himself to maintain eye contact to prevent his gaze from shifting back to the floor. Looking at her was like swimming upstream. Her skin was olive-coloured, her hair black silk.

'Everything OK?' he asked. 'Summer…?'

A thin scar ran down her neck and disappeared beneath

her blouse. The pressure in his throat increased. He hardly had time to hear her response before he disappeared into his office, backing in like a badger. Smiled apologetically at her, his face slightly crumpled. The door closed between them with an unhurried click. He sank down at his desk, resisted the impulse to put his face in his hands. A withered and unredeemed sensation reverberated through him. He quickly stifled the thought, stuffing it down into the depths.

That same afternoon he sat at his desk with one of John Donne's sermons from 1627 in front of him. The sunlight lay like a honey-yellow glaze over the dark-green lawn outside. The older students had rolled out a square plastic mat there, covered it in soap and got the new arrivals to play bandy on it barefoot. They slipped helplessly around, tumbling into one another like blind seals. Their shrill voices intermittently penetrated the quiet of Jakob's office. Each time he would jump without really noticing it. He read, so deeply engrossed in the text that his body swayed along with the rhythm of the speech:

> *They are creatures, that have not so much of a body as flesh is, as froth is, as a vapour is, as a sigh is, and yet with a touch they shall moulder a rock into less atoms, than the sand that it stands upon; and a millstone into smaller flour, than it grinds. They are creatures made, and yet not a minute elder now, than when they were first made, if they were made before all measure of time began...*

When someone knocked on his door he marked his place in the book with a finger but continued reading anyway. Another knock. He closed the book, glancing briefly inside its covers before looking up and noticing that the light had shifted and the dust within it swirled, although he'd been sitting completely still for at least fifty minutes with the same book. It's odd that it should be swirling when no one has moved, he thought, and noted furthermore that he had asked the person out there to enter, because now he came into the room. It was the lankier of his undergraduates, Filip.

'Yes?' said Jakob, and the student stopped himself midway to sitting on the chair opposite him.

'I have my tutorial with you now, twenty to two,' he said, first a little hesitantly, but then he sat down anyway.

His eyebrows were raised, and unusually lush, thought Jakob, for someone so young. They looked sculpted, as though he had trimmed them here and there so that the hairs wouldn't be too long.

'Oh right, yes, exactly,' said Jakob, pulling his finger out of the book and pushing it aside.

It wasn't their first meeting, or their last. Certain students only came in once or twice, handled everything themselves, while others wanted to discuss the tiniest footnote, dragged out their thesis-writing for multiple terms and essentially – though they rarely realized it themselves – needed help setting limits. This Filip seemed mostly interested in having someone to listen while he expounded on his chosen subject, Gnosticism. As though to reassure himself that he'd understood it correctly or perhaps, it struck Jakob, that his adviser had sufficient knowledge of the subject. Filip was an art historian and seemed sceptical of all other disciplines.

'So how's it going?' Jakob asked, and wondered if fifteen minutes was too little time to devote to this, if he should extend it to twenty.

Filip launched in without the slightest sense of urgency and asked no questions. Most male students began to dress like English professors by the time they had completed a couple of terms, Jakob thought as he listened to Filip. Tweed jackets, or at least some material that resembled tweed, with patches on the elbows. But not this one. He wore jeans with several holes and a green T-shirt with some kind of axe logo and the words 'What would Raskolnikov do?' He was grey-eyed, brown-haired, and sat like a cricket. As though he'd needed to put some thought into how to fold his legs together in an acceptable manner. His knees pointed upward just a little too much. Those legs really were unusually long.

Jakob slid back in his chair and tossed in a question about methods, while wondering if the point was to bed girls or enhance some future drug trip. These days, with so many things to choose from, how come this young person – this human being before him, who presumably hadn't even moved away from home yet, presumably had parents who maybe didn't select and lay out his clothes for him every morning but surely both washed them and cooked enough Sunday meals for him to grow properly – how could it be that this young person was specifically interested in religious mysticism? When there were video games, nightclubs, trips to Australia and normal, simpler jobs. At a petrol station or a shop that provided a little pocket money which he could set aside for a bigger TV, a car or a parachute jump. Unemployment was certainly high, and it was said that people were biding their time at university, but still. Jakob couldn't believe that even half these people, who did take-home exams and attended seminars and aggregated in shapeless clumps on the wall in the smoking area during breaks, were actually interested in knowledge. The pure ground truths. He tried to avoid stereotypes, but he had a very hard time imagining that Filip, like he himself, had the *thirst*. His lips were thin and pale, moistened with saliva, his chin totally smooth as though he had no beard growth at all.

Suddenly Filip stopped. After a little exposition about the Tranströmer poem he'd quoted in his introductory paragraph nothing more came, he grew still, closed his mouth. When Jakob said nothing, Filip got to his feet and started looking through the bookshelf nearest him, the large one.

'What's your field of research again?' he asked, and pulled out a thick hardback volume from 1912 without even looking at it.

'Right now I'm making a close study of English sermons and other surviving ecclesiastical texts from the first half of the seventeenth century,' Jakob said cautiously, and could hear himself how vague that sounded.

Filip traced his finger along the spines of the books and looked around. Just as Jakob tried to conclude by saying that Filip maybe ought to leave the introduction for now and instead finish writing the main section first, he noticed that Filip's eyes had fixed on something lying on top of the bookshelf. Half hidden behind a dead potted plant. Filip took a small step to his right and craned his neck. Then he lowered his head again and a little smile flitted across his face.

'Really,' he said. 'Interesting.'

Jakob blushed when he remembered what was up there. He quickly turned back to his computer and pulled up his work documents, pretended to glance through the first few lines. From the corner of his eye he watched Filip stand there for a few seconds before he collected his things, said that he'd email over his theory and methodology section, thanked him and left.

When the door had closed Jakob stood up and pulled out a chair so that he could climb up and take down the statue. It was smooth and cool in his hand. He used his thumb to wipe off the layer of dust that had collected on its head and shoulders. The face was mild but powerful. It was Uriel, one of the archangels. Under his arm he held a book, which symbolized wisdom. When he was a child, Uriel had been his favourite. Jakob's mother had brought it along the only time she had visited him in his office. She had found it in the attic, she said. 'Thought your office might be a good place for it.' He had placed the statue on the top shelf because he didn't want it on his desk. Then he'd forgotten about it.

In his childhood home it had been kept in a red wooden box along with two knights (one astride a horse), four plastic soldiers and a semi-transparent walrus made of blue glass. When he positioned them on the floor facing each other in attack formation the angel had looked monstrously large by comparison. Still, it always did battle alongside the walrus. They were both of another kind. The walrus had eventually been reclaimed by his mother, who had understandably been a little protective of it, and then the angel had been left to face the humans alone. He didn't remember who won the war, just how he'd lined them up. Face to face. The little ones versus the large one, who just held on to his book and stared directly at the enemy.

His mother once said of the angel that people often didn't remember Uriel. Gabriel, Michael and Raphael were named more often. His father said nothing. Neither about that nor about anything else.

He'd had a heart attack. Jakob was six years old and hadn't understood until much later. His mother had said that his father was 'away' and then, he couldn't quite remember where or when, she'd begun saying that he was 'gone'. Since his father had rarely been home, the change was barely notice-able. His mother started smoking under the extractor hood above the stove rather than out on the balcony. That was it.

His father had a belt, which he'd once used to tie her hands together and hang them from a hook, leaving her standing on her toes, her arms extended, unable to get down. Then he'd left.

Jakob had stood in the doorway between his room and the kitchen, and his mother had screamed at him to get away from there. First his name, three times, with a disintegrating voice.

'Jakob! Jakob! Jakob!'

And then commanded him.

'Go to your room!'

She had screamed it over her shoulder, with her back to him. The whites of her eyes shone like those of a trapped animal. Not long after that his father died. Fell headlong onto the floor.

Jakob went home early from the university that day, jogged down the stairs. Stopped with his fingers a few centimetres from the light-grey keypad by the entry door.

Donne.

He had forgotten the book in his office, returned it to the

shelf with the others. He stood there for an instant. A free evening. A walk. Maybe a film?

No. He turned and walked back.

The long corridor was quiet, a few colleagues working with their doors open. He didn't make eye contact, didn't want to chat, didn't want anyone to notice that he was going home so early. Not even Lucy. Instead he let the familiar dark-grey floor tiles escort him. Moved like a shadow, rounding the corner almost silently.

But someone was there, also quick and quiet. They collided forcefully. He took the impact on the right side of his chest, buckled, but had time to steady himself against the wall. She fell straight backwards. Her arms flew up so that she dropped her things, papers, a pencil case, two books. A new faculty member, he thought, but then he saw the round face. The black pageboy haircut was a mess. She clutched one elbow and winced. He helped her up.

'Are you OK?' asked Jakob.

She nodded and together they collected her things. He recognized the books from one of his reading lists. She was short, surely not more than one metre sixty, with light-blue eyes and something about her that was vaguely like an overgrown baby. A little chubby, the back of her hands rounded, short fingers, pale porcelain skin against the dark hair.

'Thanks,' she said, and straightened her clothes. 'Via Dolorosa!'

A joking smile. Then she was gone.

He stood there for a moment and briefly touched his hand to the point of impact. Picked up his briefcase and walked to his office. He pulled out the key.

But the door was unlocked. He stepped in and turned on the light, locked the door behind him to compensate, walked to the shelf and pulled out the book. A little slip of paper fell to the floor. He bent down and picked it up. Rounded in form, glossy underneath. A collectible bookmark. He turned it over.

It was a cherub.

He dropped it as though it had burned him. In the same moment the precious Donne book slid out of his hands, landed on the stone floor and fell open with a whimper that turned his stomach. When he picked it up he saw that a portion of the spine had come loose. He nearly burst into tears.

The cherub had stuck to his jacket sleeve.

With a mildly disgusted expression he pulled it loose. Held the scrap of paper by its leg in his index finger and thumb, with the very tips of his fingers. The little boy was naked except for a light-blue cloth that billowed between his hands and down in an arc in front of his genitals. It was apparent that the picture was of a child, but something in the round face and portly stomach was more suggestive of a rather fat adult man. The cherub was in mid-stride, as though taking part in a circle dance. Its eyelids were lowered, giving it a dull demeanour, and its gaze was directed slightly to the right. The legs were short, plump. It looked like it might stumble at any moment. Sections of the paint on its golden locks had rubbed off so that they looked greyish. Shabby. The wings were small and pink-hued and placed way too far out on the shoulders.

It must've been Filip, thought Jakob, Filip who'd hatched this ingenious idea that truly shone with comic brilliance, to pilfer one of his little sister's old bookmarks. Surely he joked about him with his friends. Sat in the student bar on campus and sniggered about him. *That old angel idiot*. To upset him, throw him off balance. It was a lucky shot, in many ways.

Jakob had always despised these chubby little childish nudes with their puffed-out cheeks. Lazing about, strumming instruments on some billowing cloud. The ones that everyday people foolishly assumed could even belong in the *same league* as the soft-spoken, secretive ones. Those who cannot be looked upon directly by humans. Impossible to take in, to comprehend.

Goddamned swine, those students.

Autumn came late that year, it didn't get cold until the end of October. Jakob's apartment was in a tall suburban high-rise with walls as thick as a castle's. On the seventh floor, beyond the reach of the trees. As far up as he could get. The crows often circled the building with their echoing, hollow calls. Sometimes he saw them on the ground, frozen in a pointed pose, fixing their eyes on him until he had passed. Cold black eyes, grey-black uniform and shiny leather shoes.

He put the bags down in the lift, pressed the button and wiped the rain from his face. Fumbled for his keys.

With the radio on he cooked some food. The illuminated kitchen shone out into the night. The rain began to drum against the window. The closer to winter, the more the light in there seemed to shine. From outside he'd be completely visible, but no one could see him because he lived so high up. He pulled the pot off the stove, removed the oven glove and turned off the fan.

He ate, washed up. Left the radio on. Outside the window it started to snow.

*

Later everything had grown quiet. He lay in his bedroom. From the corner of his eye he watched the clock radio's red digits count the minutes.

When he closed his eyes he tried to conjure a vision of something slowly approaching him. He tried to distinguish a figure, facial features, but nothing came to him. It never had, since that one time. Dreams were only normal images now. Banal remains of the day. What he thought had been the prelude to a breakthrough had gone silent. Time and time again he read through old notes, he knew the oldest sections by heart. Searched for something without knowing what. As though the meaning would one day emerge from between the sentences. Smiling at him in the white darkness.

Every night, in the interlude before falling asleep, he leaned into the void from his side and fumbled with his hands in front of him, feeling for something that he hoped was also leaning in somewhere, from the opposite side. When he closed his eyes all he saw was the dull colour of nothingness. That was exactly how he pictured the gap, the tear in the fabric. In those spots where nothing existed, that's where *something else* could exist. One of those mighty, secretive beings. The one that left all human proportions behind.

The liminal creature.

When sleep came he walked blindly right into the darkness. But once again no voice spoke to him. No one came.

'How goes it?'

Lucy stood in the doorway with a bundle of papers. She was wearing her hair down. It had grown a lot since he'd last seen her. She had been gone for two weeks, maybe she'd been ill. Or out of the country, on holiday. Swimming in the ocean. Jakob had sat down in the corner armchair to rest for a moment. The clock above her head read half past four. Had he been sitting there for an hour?

'It's OK,' said Jakob, straightening his back. 'Or rather, I have... a bit of a problem with a student.'

She stepped in and discreetly closed the door behind her. Today she wore pressed navy-blue trousers and a white blouse. Had she ever been in his office before? Completely inside, her whole body, not just a foot or a head? He didn't recall. But now she was. He stood up, pushed up his glasses and massaged the spot between his eyes a bit.

Lucy stood by the door and waited, so he continued.

'It started as a joke, I think. But now it's progressed to, well, almost harassment.'

'Do you know which student is involved?'

There was a new smell in the room, which she must've brought with her. Lotion, he guessed. She probably had an expensive cream in her handbag which she used whenever she felt like it. A mild vanilla scent with a nutty undertone.

'I thought it would stop if I just waited them out, that they'd tire of it.'

He moved towards her, stopping a few steps away.

'So there's more than one?'

'I'll show you,' said Jakob. 'You'll see, I have it all saved in a folder. I thought if I needed proof some day, then I'd have it.'

He produced a black folder from the bookshelf. Lucy was still standing near the door so he edged closer as he opened it. Nine of them, glued across a two-page spread.

'I don't really understand,' Lucy said after a moment.

'They're cherubs,' said Jakob, closing the folder with a little slap.

She looked at him sideways, he could feel it. She didn't like the winter, he'd heard her say so in the staffroom. Always felt the cold. 'No coat is warm enough for me.' It had been a long time now since she was last picked up after work. Several weeks since that man last walked in and leaned against her door frame.

'Do the students send you bookmarks?' said Lucy.

'Not send,' he said. 'They hide them. In here.'

She looked slowly around.

'Where?'

He made a sweeping movement with his hand.

'Everywhere. Under the mouse pad, in the bookshelf or in one of the drawers. They've got cleverer and cleverer...'

He suddenly felt her hand on his arm. The warmth penetrated the shirt fabric and right into his bloodstream. Her fingers weren't cold at all.

'Can I help you somehow?' she said.

He stood there quietly, stole a glance at her thin wrist. Heard a distant clicking sound that he couldn't place.

'Thanks,' he said. 'But that's not necessary.'

She squeezed his forearm lightly, then she said she had to go.

As soon as she left, Jakob held his arm to his face. There it was, the scent of Lucy. He drew in a steady stream of air while making his way to his chair and tossed the folder on his desk. It fell open. He shuffled a little further forward and kept smelling his arm, growing dizzy from all the oxygen but not letting that stop him. Just in front of him the folder lay open.

A swathe of pink and light blue, a few puffy white clouds and various gilded instruments. He was disgusted but couldn't look away. Naked flesh. Rounded faces. *No structure, just shapes.* A different face flickered past. The cherubs' eyelids were alternately half closed and wide open. Chubby, malformed, all staring at him. The vanilla scent in his nose, the dizziness. Everything intensified for an instant. Then he let his arm fall.

He stood up so quickly that everything went black; he fumbled for the folder in the darkness, and when his vision returned he began tearing at the pictures. Clawing them loose, tearing with his nails like a lunatic. The desktop filled with paper scraps until only one remained glued into the folder. When he raked at it the picture suddenly came loose. As he crumpled it he caught a glimpse of something written on the back. In faint pencil. He unfolded the bookmark again.

Gemini geminos quaerunt.

Twins seek each other.

A little golden bell pinged when he pushed open the cafe door. He was on time and she was early, already sitting at one of the round tables further in. Smartly dressed in a dark-blue cardigan and grey wool skirt. The radio was playing American Christmas music. He ordered four different little pastries and two cups of black coffee. It was a tradition they shared, one of only a few.

When he reached the table he set down the tray. The chair scraped against the floor as she stood. They briefly hugged.

'Hi, Mum.'

She still lived in the same apartment, several miles away. When she occasionally turned up in Jakob's thoughts she was always so tactile, sticky. Came towards him with weepy eyes and sweaty hands. It almost turned his stomach and he would quickly force her away again. In reality she was different. Reserved, withdrawn. Jaded.

They sat down, sipped their coffee in silence for a moment.

'How are things at the university?' she asked, and cut off a bit of pastry with her teaspoon. 'Is it going all right?'

He had met Lucy near the coffee machine the day before and said hello, but she had just given him a slight nod, taken a glass of water and gone.

'Everything's fine,' said Jakob. 'All good.'

His mother hesitated with her spoon halfway to her mouth, then lowered it. Her grey hair seemed lighter than the last time, her face more sunken.

'And financially?'

It was as if she could smell her way to it.

'I told you, everything's fine.'

There were only a few weeks left before his position expired. He had applied for grants, pestered Harald about hourly work. 'I am valued as a teacher. You know that. Ask the students. Ask them!' It was as though all his words and efforts, all the forms, all the letters he'd sent had just got sucked up and disappeared. Rejections. He even knew already who was going to get his office. Or rather, he guessed. She had prowled by a few times like a scavenger, eyeing the space with sidelong glances.

His plate remained untouched. The cream started to run out of one of the pastries like a viscous river. A dark band of chocolate held it together like a noose.

'Did Dad use to...' He cleared his throat, gathering momentum. 'Did he ever, you know, hurt you?'

'What kind of nonsense are you talking about?' his mother replied immediately. Washed down another mouthful with coffee.

'I only remember that time' – Jakob lowered his voice a bit – 'with the belt.'

She stared at him. He could sense it despite the fact that his eyes remained fixed on the little candleholder in the middle of the chequered tablecloth between them.

'Where do you get that from?' she said.

Then he looked up, expecting to see her looking sad. But she looked more irritated than anything else.

'Have you met anyone yet?' she retorted.

Nibbled at him with her big teeth like a horse.

'How do you mean?' he asked.

'A woman. Have you met a woman?'

Several times he'd fantasized about lying. Yes, Mum. I've met a woman who is beautiful and intelligent. She is so beautiful that people turn around when she passes them on the street. She has a skirt that breaks like waves against her legs. She has a high, pale forehead. And she chose me. I'm the one she chose, Mum.

'Oh, that. No.'

'That would cheer you up,' she said, and scraped up the last bits from her plate. 'It's started getting so dark in the evenings now. Black as night.'

'One day the night turns white,' said Jakob, looking out at the dusk.

Slush and hurried feet in winter boots. Advent candles on the windowsill.

'"Don't be afraid,"' his mother sang. '"There is a sign, a secret…"'

It startled him. A little coffee splashed out of his cup and dripped onto his trousers.

'What did you say?'

'I didn't say anything,' she said. 'I'm singing.'

'Well, what are you singing, then?'

She sang on in her thin, metallic, clear voice.

'"You're on your way, one day the night turns white. One day and stars will grow within His arms. Don't be afraid, there is a harbour here. In darkness still for you, but you will see."'

Jakob's body was full of stones that shattered. And shattered.

'A hymn,' he said.

'Ylva Eggehorn wrote it, I think,' said his mother. 'I played it for you when you were little. Amazing what a memory you've got, after all!'

'Truly,' said Jakob, and closed his eyes.

There wasn't much left any more. If there had ever been anything. He couldn't sleep, lay wide awake in the darkness. The quilt was neither too hot nor too cold, just nothing. Rain fell against the glass. The night was so black that he ought to be able to fall asleep with his eyes open. It made no difference. But it didn't work. He'd been lying there for hours.

Eventually he got up.

He wrapped his robe around himself and walked down the dark hallway to the bathroom. Turned on the light. The fluorescent tubes blinked to life and then shone steadily. He squinted. Sat down with the weight of a thousand kilos on the toilet, a pitiful trickling sound in the water.

After he'd flushed he turned out the light and went to the kitchen to drink some water. He switched on the single ceiling light and managed to turn the tap too far, so that cold drops splashed inside the V-neck of his dressing gown. He saw himself reflected in the kitchen window.

Without his glasses he looked like a stranger.

All of a sudden he felt it clearly. That the only thing to emerge from the recurring dream he'd had since childhood had done so haltingly, squinting into the light after a long journey underground. Finally found an opening in the bed-rock. But once outside, nothing awaited it.

Nothing at all. Just think how simple it had been the whole time.

If only he'd known.

He went closer to the window. His eyes looked like caves. Behind them only darkness. He turned out the light in order to see outside. The night was black as oil. Far below he imagined the winter-bare birch branches beating against each other in the wind. He carefully leaned his forehead against the cold glass. The rain streamed past and he stood like that for a little while. His tears welled up, throat tightening like a blocked drain. His breathing was rapid and the sorrow racked him against his will; he tried to choke it back but it climbed up his throat. *Nothing will be all right.* There was no strength left to prevent it. His forehead slid down, his body swayed. He had to brace himself with his palms against the glass to keep from falling.

But then.

A movement in the darkness above the rooftops. Just outside. He slowly raised his head.

There it was.

Bigger than he could have ever imagined. Grey-blue, almost black. The small eyes set far apart on either side of the jutting head. A long line formed the slightly smiling mouth. Further down the sides, two long, flat fins in slow rotation. He couldn't look at the whole thing at once, it was too big. His eyes weren't enough. It emitted a strange clicking sound that grew stronger. As if someone was dragging a coin along his vertebrae. It came closer and closer, stretching to its full length along the wall. Just across from him, on the other side of the glass. Must be taller than the whole building. A little portion of the left side of its face took up his whole window.

He looked right into its eye.

Saw the pupil constrict. An ancient eyelid opening and closing. He could distinguish individual eyelashes. Jakob's breathing was heavy. All the oxygen made him dizzy. It looked human. Against the black night the white of its eye shone at him like sunlit silver. *The silver gaze*. Then it began to sing. An underwater song from the deep. Something shifted inside Jakob. Something happened. A warmth flowed through him, began to surge. His body relaxed.

And for just a moment he allowed himself to be dazzled.

Translator's Note

The grandeur of the Italian Alps occupied an uncredited title role in *Snow, Dog, Foot*, the subject of last year's Peirene Stevns Translation Prize. Similarly, the human stories in the book you now hold are inextricably linked to evocative surroundings. Andrea Lundgren's *Nordic Fauna* is rooted not simply in the Swedish language, with its particular economy, pacing and rhythm, but also in Sweden itself. Norrbotten more specifically, Sweden's largest, most northerly and least populous county. In this context, references to animals, forests and waterways carry culturally layered meaning. Conveying a sufficiently nuanced version of this iconic Swedish landscape was a delightful challenge.

I am grateful for the opportunity to immerse myself in this text and for the responsibility of rendering Lundgren's finely wrought short stories into engaging English while remaining faithful to her depictions of human struggles with identity, regret, vulnerability, truth and our place among our fellow creatures. I have relished constructing the appropriate English version of Swedish concepts, both when corresponding words were available and when the phrase or structure was uniquely Lundgren's. That process, coupled with each story's excursions into magical realism, has made for a truly rich experience. It is remarkable how shepherding a two-word sentence and its associated punctuation can consume as much effort as a paragraph of text. To that end I deeply appreciate Sarah Death's patient mentorship and the keen editorial eyes of Gesche Ipsen and Lesley Levene, who added clarity and nuance in all the right places, tactfully steering my drafts towards their final form. Stella Sabin and Maddie Rogers at Peirene Press have been welcoming and supportive beyond my expectations.

This work has been an opportunity to accomplish a long-standing professional goal. As a debut project I am fortunate to have been charged with translating a collection of short stories, each of which provided its own intricacies and challenges. As a native speaker of Swedish and English, I have appreciated the experience of encountering my limitations in both languages and devising the most effective way to overcome them. The whole undertaking could not have happened without the strength and support of my partner, Dr Britt Erickson, and the laughter of our daughter, Ida.

The emergence and global spread of a novel coronavirus constrained the pace of life during much of my work on this book, precluding me from the luxury of single-minded focus on the translation. I had looked forward to that productive solitude. Instead, like all of you, I have been forced to adapt to isolation amid so much uncertainty and grief. This moment in history has thrown our interconnectedness into stark relief, exposing the frailty of our individual bodies as well as our institutions, our empathy and our social cohesion. Thanks to the richness of Lundgren's stories, my time spent engaged with this inward-looking text has come as a welcome respite from daily clinical work confronting the stark realities of the pandemic.

I deeply appreciate Martha Stevns's insight and generosity in providing aspiring translators the opportunity to do meaningful work, learn from the best and find a path forward. Although public health restrictions prevented me from retreating to the Pyrenees as the prize specifies, Martha's generous gift will instead become a welcome escape for me and my family one year hence. By then, with any luck, the world will have reached a new balance point after far too many months spent mired in disease, conflict and loss.

I hope that you will enjoy this book as much as I have. More broadly, I hope for all of us that Andrea Lundgren's empathetic prose, and these fraught times, will call to mind this excerpt from Lynn Ungar's recent poem 'Pandemic':

> *Know that we are connected*
> *in ways that are terrifying and beautiful.*

JOHN LITELL

Subscribe

Discover the best of contemporary European literature: subscribe to Peirene Press and receive a world-class novella from us three times a year, direct to your door. The books are sent out six weeks before they are available in bookshops and online.

Your subscription will allow us to plan ahead with confidence and help us to continue to introduce English readers to the joy of new foreign literature for many years to come.

'A class act'

THE GUARDIAN

'Two-hour books to be devoured in a single sitting: literary cinema for those fatigued by film'

TIMES LITERARY SUPPLEMENT

A one year subscription costs £35 (3 books, free p&p for UK)

Please sign up via our online shop at
www.peirenepress.com/shop